EX LIBRIS

NAME

※ A Series of Unfortunate Events ※

BOOK the Third

THE WIDE WINDOW

by LEMONY SNICKET

Illustrations by Brett Helquist

▆ HarperCollinsPublishers

The Wide Window

Text copyright © 2000 by Lemony Snicket
Illustrations copyright © 2000 by Brett Helquist

Library of Congress Cataloging-in-Publication Data
Snicket, Lemony.
    The wide window / by Lemony Snicket ; illustrations by Brett Helquist.
        p.   cm. — (A series of unfortunate events ; bk. 3)
    Summary: Catastrophes and misfortune continue to plague the Baudelaire
orphans after they're sent to live with fearful Aunt Josephine who offers little
protection against Count Olaf's treachery.
    ISBN 0-06-440768-3 (paper-over-board) — ISBN 0-06-028314-9 (lib. bdg.)
    [1. Orphans—Fiction.   2. Brothers and sisters—Fiction.   3. Humorous
stories.]   I. Helquist, Brett, ill.   II. Title.   III. Series: Snicket, Lemony.
Series of unfortunate events ; bk. 3.
PZ7.S6795Wi   2000   99-27262
[Fic]—dc21   CIP

Typography by Margaret Wagner
1   2   3   4   5   6   7   8   9   10   ❖   First Edition
Visit us on the World Wide Web! http://www.harperchildrens.com

For Beatrice—
I would much prefer it if you were alive and well.

C H A P T E R
One

If you didn't know much about the Baudelaire orphans, and you saw them sitting on their suitcases at Damocles Dock, you might think that they were bound for an exciting adventure. After all, the three children had just disembarked from the Fickle Ferry, which had driven them across Lake Lachrymose to live with their Aunt Josephine, and in most cases such a situation would lead to thrillingly good times.

But of course you would be dead wrong. For although Violet, Klaus, and Sunny Baudelaire were about to experience events that would be both exciting and memorable, they would not be exciting and memorable like having your fortune told or going to a rodeo. Their adventure would be exciting and memorable like being chased by a werewolf through a field of thorny bushes at midnight with nobody around to help you. If you are interested in reading a story filled with thrillingly good times, I am sorry to inform you that you are most certainly reading the wrong book, because the Baudelaires experience very few good times over the course of their gloomy and miserable lives. It is a terrible thing, their misfortune, so terrible that I can scarcely bring myself to write about it. So if you do not want to read a story of tragedy and sadness, this is your very last chance to put this book down, because the misery of the Baudelaire orphans begins in the very next paragraph.

"Look what I have for you," Mr. Poe said, grinning from ear to ear and holding out a small paper bag. "Peppermints!" Mr. Poe was a banker who had been placed in charge of handling the affairs of the Baudelaire orphans after their parents died. Mr. Poe was kindhearted, but it is not enough in this world to be kindhearted, particularly if you are responsible for keeping children out of danger. Mr. Poe had known the three children since they were born, and could never remember that they were allergic to peppermints.

"Thank you, Mr. Poe," Violet said, and took the paper bag and peered inside. Like most fourteen-year-olds, Violet was too well mannered to mention that if she ate a peppermint she would break out in hives, a phrase which here means "be covered in red, itchy rashes for a few hours." Besides, she was too occupied with inventing thoughts to pay much attention to Mr. Poe. Anyone who knew Violet would know that when her hair was tied up in a ribbon to keep it out of her eyes, the way it was now, her thoughts were filled with wheels, gears, levers, and other necessary things for inventions. At this particular moment she was thinking of how she could improve the engine of the Fickle Ferry so it wouldn't belch smoke into the gray sky.

"That's very kind of you," said Klaus, the middle Baudelaire child, smiling at Mr. Poe and thinking that if he had even one lick of a peppermint, his tongue would swell up and he would scarcely be able to speak. Klaus took his glasses off and wished that Mr. Poe had bought him a book or a newspaper instead. Klaus was a voracious reader, and when he had learned about his allergy at a birthday party when he was eight, he had immediately read all his parents' books about allergies. Even four years later he could recite the chemical formulas that caused his tongue to swell up.

"Toi!" Sunny shrieked. The youngest Baudelaire was only an infant, and like many infants, she spoke mostly in words that were tricky to understand. By "Toi!" she probably meant "I have never eaten a peppermint because I suspect that I, like my siblings, am allergic to them," but it was hard to tell. She may also have meant "I wish I could bite a peppermint, because I like to bite things with my four sharp teeth, but I don't want to risk an allergic reaction."

"You can eat them on your cab ride to Mrs. Anwhistle's house," Mr. Poe said, coughing into his white handkerchief. Mr. Poe always seemed to have a cold and the Baudelaire orphans were accustomed to receiving information from him between bouts of hacking and wheezing. "She apologizes for not meeting you at the dock, but she says she's frightened of it."

"Why would she be frightened of a dock?" Klaus asked, looking around at the wooden piers and sailboats.

"She's frightened of anything to do with Lake Lachrymose," Mr. Poe said, "but she didn't say why. Perhaps it has to do with her husband's death. Your Aunt Josephine—she's not really your aunt, of course; she's your second cousin's sister-in-law, but asked that you call her Aunt Josephine—your Aunt Josephine lost her husband recently, and it may be possible that he drowned or died in a boat accident. It didn't seem polite to ask how she became a dowager. Well, let's put you in a taxi."

"What does that word mean?" Violet asked.

Mr. Poe looked at Violet and raised his eyebrows. "I'm surprised at you, Violet," he said. "A girl of your age should know that a taxi is a car which will drive you someplace for a fee. Now, let's gather your luggage and walk to the curb."

"'Dowager,'" Klaus whispered to Violet, "is a fancy word for 'widow.'"

"Thank you," she whispered back, picking up her suitcase in one hand and Sunny in the other. Mr. Poe was waving his handkerchief in the air to signal a taxi to stop, and in no time at all the cabdriver piled all of the Baudelaire suitcases into the trunk and Mr. Poe piled the Baudelaire children into the back seat.

"I will say good-bye to you here," Mr. Poe said. "The banking day has already begun, and I'm afraid if I go with you out to Aunt

Josephine's I will never get anything done. Please give her my best wishes, and tell her that I will keep in touch regularly." Mr. Poe paused for a moment to cough into his handkerchief before continuing. "Now, your Aunt Josephine is a bit nervous about having three children in her house, but I assured her that you three were very well behaved. Make sure you mind your manners, and, as always, you can call or fax me at the bank if there's any sort of problem. Although I don't imagine anything will go wrong *this* time."

When Mr. Poe said "*this* time," he looked at the children meaningfully as if it were their fault that poor Uncle Monty was dead. But the Baudelaires were too nervous about meeting their new caretaker to say anything more to Mr. Poe except "So long."

"So long," Violet said, putting the bag of peppermints in her pocket.

"So long," Klaus said, taking one last look at Damocles Dock.

"Frul!" Sunny shrieked, chewing on her seat belt buckle.

"So long," Mr. Poe replied, "and good luck to you. I will think of the Baudelaires as often as I can."

Mr. Poe gave some money to the taxi driver and waved good-bye to the three children as the cab pulled away from the dock and onto a gray, cobblestoned street. There was a small grocery store with barrels of limes and beets out front. There was a clothing store called Look! It Fits!, which appeared to be undergoing renovations. There was a terrible-looking restaurant called the Anxious Clown, with neon lights and balloons in the window. But mostly, there were many stores and shops that were all closed up, with boards or metal gratings over the windows and doors.

"The town doesn't seem very crowded," Klaus remarked. "I was hoping we might make some new friends here."

"It's the off-season," the cabdriver said. He

was a skinny man with a skinny cigarette hanging out of his mouth, and as he talked to the children he looked at them through the rearview mirror. "The town of Lake Lachrymose is a resort, and when the nice weather comes it's as crowded as can be. But around now, things here are as dead as the cat I ran over this morning. To make new friends, you'll have to wait until the weather gets a little better. Speaking of which, Hurricane Herman is expected to arrive in town in a week or so. You better make sure you have enough food up there in the house."

"A hurricane on a lake?" Klaus asked. "I thought hurricanes only occurred near the ocean."

"A body of water as big as Lake Lachrymose," the driver said, "can have anything occur on it. To tell you the truth, I'd be a little nervous about living on top of this hill. Once the storm hits, it'll be very difficult to drive all the way down into town."

Violet, Klaus, and Sunny looked out the window and saw what the driver meant by "all the way down." The taxi had turned one last corner and arrived at the scraggly top of a tall, tall hill, and the children could see the town far, far below them, the cobblestone road curling around the buildings like a tiny gray snake, and the small square of Damocles Dock with specks of people bustling around it. And out beyond the dock was the inky blob of Lake Lachrymose, huge and dark as if a monster were standing over the three orphans, casting a giant shadow below them. For a few moments the children stared into the lake as if hypnotized by this enormous stain on the landscape.

"The lake is so enormous," Klaus said, "and it looks so deep. I can almost understand why Aunt Josephine is afraid of it."

"The lady who lives up here," the cabdriver asked, "is afraid of the lake?"

"That's what we've been told," Violet said.

The cabdriver shook his head and brought

the cab to a halt. "I don't know how she can stand it, then."

"What do you mean?" Violet asked.

"You mean you've never been to this house?" he asked.

"No, never," Klaus replied. "We've never even met our Aunt Josephine before."

"Well, if your Aunt Josephine is afraid of the water," the cabdriver said, "I can't believe she lives here in this house."

"What are you talking about?" Klaus asked.

"Well, take a look," the driver answered, and got out of the cab.

The Baudelaires took a look. At first, the three youngsters saw only a small boxy square with a peeling white door, and it looked as if the house was scarcely bigger than the taxi which had taken them to it. But as they piled out of the car and drew closer, they saw that this small square was the only part of the house that was on top of the hill. The rest of it—a large pile of boxy squares, all stuck together like ice cubes—

hung over the side, attached to the hill by long metal stilts that looked like spider legs. As the three orphans peered down at their new home, it seemed as if the entire house were holding on to the hill for dear life.

The taxi driver took their suitcases out of the trunk, set them in front of the peeling white door, and drove down the hill with a *toot!* of his horn for a good-bye. There was a soft squeak as the peeling white door opened, and from behind the door appeared a pale woman with her white hair piled high on top of her head in a bun.

"Hello," she said, smiling thinly. "I'm your Aunt Josephine."

"Hello," Violet said, cautiously, and stepped forward to meet her new guardian. Klaus stepped forward behind her, and Sunny crawled forward behind him, but all three Baudelaires were walking carefully, as if their weight would send the house toppling down from its perch.

The orphans couldn't help wondering how a woman who was so afraid of Lake Lachrymose could live in a house that felt like it was about to fall into its depths.

"*This* is the radiator," Aunt Josephine said, pointing to a radiator with a pale and skinny finger. "Please don't ever touch it. You may find yourself very cold here in my home. I never turn on the radiator, because I am frightened that it might explode, so it often gets chilly in the evenings."

Violet and Klaus looked at one another briefly, and Sunny looked at both of them. Aunt Josephine was giving them a tour of their new home and so far appeared to be afraid of everything in it, from the welcome mat—which, Aunt Josephine explained, could cause someone to trip and break their neck—to the sofa in the living room, which she said could fall over at any time and crush them flat.

"This is the telephone," Aunt Josephine said, gesturing to the telephone. "It should only be used in emergencies, because there is a danger of electrocution."

"Actually," Klaus said, "I've read quite a bit about electricity. I'm pretty sure that the telephone is perfectly safe."

Aunt Josephine's hands fluttered to her white hair as if something had jumped onto her head. "You can't believe everything you read," she pointed out.

"I've built a telephone from scratch," Violet said. "If you'd like, I could take the telephone apart and show you how it works. That might make you feel better."

"I don't think so," Aunt Josephine said, frowning.

"Delmo!" Sunny offered, which probably meant something along the lines of "If you wish, I will bite the telephone to show you that it's harmless."

"Delmo?" Aunt Josephine asked, bending over to pick up a piece of lint from the faded flowery carpet. "What do you mean by 'delmo'? I consider myself an expert on the English language, and I have no idea what the word 'delmo' means. Is she speaking some other language?"

"Sunny doesn't speak fluently yet, I'm afraid," Klaus said, picking his little sister up. "Just baby talk, mostly."

"Grun!" Sunny shrieked, which meant something like "I object to your calling it baby talk!"

"Well, I will have to teach her proper English," Aunt Josephine said stiffly. "I'm sure you all need some brushing up on your grammar, actually. Grammar is the greatest joy in life, don't you find?"

The three siblings looked at one another. Violet was more likely to say that inventing things was the greatest joy in life, Klaus thought reading was, and Sunny of course took no greater pleasure than in biting things. The Baudelaires thought of grammar—all those rules about how to write and speak the English language—the way they thought of banana bread: fine, but nothing to make a fuss about. Still, it seemed rude to contradict Aunt Josephine.

"Yes," Violet said finally. "We've always loved grammar."

Aunt Josephine nodded, and gave the Baudelaires a small smile. "Well, I'll show you to your room and continue the rest of the tour after dinner. When you open this door, just push on the wood here. Never use the doorknob. I'm always afraid that it will shatter into a million pieces and that one of them will hit my eye."

The Baudelaires were beginning to think that they would not be allowed to touch a single object in the whole house, but they smiled at Aunt Josephine, pushed on the wood, and opened the door to reveal a large, well-lit room with blank white walls and a plain blue carpet on the floor. Inside were two good-sized beds and one good-sized crib, obviously for Sunny, each covered in a plain blue bedspread, and at the foot of each bed was a large trunk, for storing things. At the other end of the room was a large closet for everyone's clothes, a small window for looking out, and a medium-sized pile of tin cans for no apparent purpose.

"I'm sorry that all three of you have to share a room," Aunt Josephine said, "but this house isn't very big. I tried to provide you with everything you would need, and I do hope you will be comfortable."

"I'm sure we will," Violet said, carrying her suitcase into the room. "Thank you very much, Aunt Josephine."

"In each of your trunks," Aunt Josephine said, "there is a present."

Presents? The Baudelaires had not received presents for a long, long time. Smiling, Aunt Josephine walked to the first trunk and opened it. "For Violet," she said, "there is a lovely new doll with plenty of outfits for it to wear." Aunt Josephine reached inside and pulled out a plastic doll with a tiny mouth and wide, staring eyes. "Isn't she adorable? Her name is Pretty Penny."

"Oh, thank you," said Violet, who at fourteen was too old for dolls and had never particularly liked dolls anyway. Forcing a smile on her face, she took Pretty Penny from Aunt Josephine and patted it on its little plastic head.

"And for Klaus," Aunt Josephine said, "there is a model train set." She opened the second trunk and pulled out a tiny train car. "You can set up the tracks in that empty corner of the room."

"What fun," said Klaus, trying to look excited. Klaus had never liked model trains, as they were a lot of work to put together and when you were done all you had was something that went around and around in endless circles.

"And for little Sunny," Aunt Josephine said,

reaching into the smallest trunk, which sat at the foot of the crib, "here is a rattle. See, Sunny, it makes a little noise."

Sunny smiled at Aunt Josephine, showing all four of her sharp teeth, but her older siblings knew that Sunny despised rattles and the irritating sounds they made when you shook them. Sunny had been given a rattle when she was very small, and it was the only thing she was not sorry to lose in the enormous fire that had destroyed the Baudelaire home.

"It is so generous of you," Violet said, "to give us all of these things." She was too polite to add that they weren't things they particularly liked.

"Well, I am very happy to have you here," Aunt Josephine said. "I love grammar so much. I'm excited to be able to share my love of grammar with three nice children like yourselves. Well, I'll give you a few minutes to settle in and then we'll have some dinner. See you soon."

"Aunt Josephine," Klaus asked, "what are these cans for?"

"Those cans? For burglars, naturally," Aunt Josephine said, patting the bun of hair on top of her head. "You must be as frightened of burglars as I am. So every night, simply place these tin cans right by the door, so that when burglars come in, they'll trip over the cans and you'll wake up."

"But what will we do then, when we're awake in a room with an angry burglar?" Violet asked. "I would prefer to sleep through a burglary."

Aunt Josephine's eyes grew wide with fear. "Angry burglars?" she repeated. "*Angry burglars?* Why are you talking about *angry burglars*? Are you trying to make us all even more frightened than we already are?"

"Of course not," Violet stuttered, not pointing out that Aunt Josephine was the one who had brought up the subject. "I'm sorry. I didn't mean to frighten you."

"Well, we'll say no more about it," Aunt Josephine said, looking nervously at the tin cans as if a burglar were tripping on them at that very minute. "I'll see you at the dinner table in a few minutes."

Their new guardian shut the door, and the Baudelaire orphans listened to her footsteps padding down the hallway before they spoke.

"Sunny can have Pretty Penny," Violet said, handing the doll to her sister. "The plastic is hard enough for chewing, I think."

"And you can have the model trains, Violet," Klaus said. "Maybe you can take apart the engines and invent something."

"But that leaves you with a rattle," Violet said. "That doesn't seem fair."

"Schu!" Sunny shrieked, which probably meant something along the lines of "It's been a long time since anything in our lives has felt fair."

The Baudelaires looked at one another with bitter smiles. Sunny was right. It wasn't fair that their parents had been taken away from them. It wasn't fair that the evil and revolting Count Olaf was pursuing them wherever they went, caring for nothing but their fortune. It wasn't fair that they moved from relative to relative, with terrible things happening at each of their new homes, as if the Baudelaires were riding on some horrible bus that stopped only at stations of unfairness and misery. And, of course, it certainly wasn't fair that Klaus only had a rattle to play with in his new home.

"Aunt Josephine obviously worked very hard to prepare this room for us," Violet said sadly. "She seems to be a good-hearted person. We shouldn't complain, even to ourselves."

"You're right," Klaus said, picking up his rattle and giving it a halfhearted little shake. "We shouldn't complain."

"Twee!" Sunny shrieked, which probably meant something like "Both of you are right. We shouldn't complain."

Klaus walked over to the window and looked out at the darkening landscape. The sun was beginning to set over the inky depths of Lake Lachrymose, and a cold evening wind was beginning to blow. Even from the other side of the glass Klaus could feel a small chill. "I want to complain, anyway," he said.

"Soup's on!" Aunt Josephine called from the kitchen. "Please come to dinner!"

Violet put her hand on Klaus's shoulder and gave it a little squeeze of comfort, and without another word the three Baudelaires headed back down the hallway and into the dining room. Aunt Josephine had set the table for four, providing a large cushion for Sunny and another pile of tin cans in the corner of the room, just in case burglars tried to steal their dinner.

"Normally, of course," Aunt Josephine said, "'soup's on' is an idiomatic expression that has nothing to do with soup. It simply means that dinner is ready. In this case, however, I've actually made soup."

"Oh good," Violet said. "There's nothing like hot soup on a chilly evening."

"Actually, it's not hot soup," Aunt Josephine said. "I never cook anything hot because I'm afraid of turning the stove on. It might burst into flames. I've made chilled cucumber soup for dinner."

The Baudelaires looked at one another and tried to hide their dismay. As you probably know, chilled cucumber soup is a delicacy that is best enjoyed on a very hot day. I myself once enjoyed it in Egypt while visiting a friend of mine who works as a snake charmer. When it is well prepared, chilled cucumber soup has a delicious, minty taste, cool and refreshing as if you are drinking something as well as eating it. But on a cold day, in a drafty room, chilled cucumber soup is about as welcome as a swarm of wasps at a bat mitzvah. In dead silence, the three children sat down at the table with their Aunt Josephine and did their best to force down the cold, slimy concoction. The only sound was of Sunny's four teeth chattering on her soup spoon as she ate her frigid dinner. As I'm sure you know, when no one is speaking at the dinner table, the meal seems to take hours, so it felt like much, much later when Aunt Josephine broke the silence.

"My dear husband and I never had children," she said, "because we were afraid to. But I do want you to know that I'm very happy that you're here. I am often very lonely up on this hill by myself, and when Mr. Poe wrote to me about your troubles I didn't want you to be as lonely as I was when I lost my dear Ike."

"Was Ike your husband?" Violet asked.

Aunt Josephine smiled, but she didn't look at Violet, as if she were talking more to herself than to the Baudelaires. "Yes," she said, in a far-away voice, "he was my husband, but he was much more than that. He was my best friend, my partner in grammar, and the only person I knew who could whistle with crackers in his mouth."

"Our mother could do that," Klaus said, smiling. "Her specialty was Mozart's fourteenth symphony."

"Ike's was Beethoven's fourth quartet," Aunt

Josephine replied. "Apparently it's a family characteristic."

"I'm sorry we never got to meet him," Violet said. "He sounds wonderful."

"He *was* wonderful," Aunt Josephine said, stirring her soup and blowing on it even though it was ice cold. "I was so sad when he died. I felt like I'd lost the two most special things in my life."

"Two?" Violet asked. "What do you mean?"

"I lost Ike," Aunt Josephine said, "and I lost Lake Lachrymose. I mean, I didn't really lose it, of course. It's still down in the valley. But I grew up on its shores. I used to swim in it every day. I knew which beaches were sandy and which were rocky. I knew all the islands in the middle of its waters and all the caves alongside its shore. Lake Lachrymose felt like a friend to me. But when it took poor Ike away from me I was too afraid to go near it anymore. I stopped swimming in it. I never went to the beach again. I even put away all my books about it. The only way I can bear to look at it is from the Wide Window in the library."

"Library?" Klaus asked, brightening. "You have a library?"

"Of course," Aunt Josephine said. "Where else could I keep all my books on grammar? If you've all finished with your soup, I'll show you the library."

"I couldn't eat another bite," Violet said truthfully.

"Irm!" Sunny shrieked in agreement.

"No, no, Sunny," Aunt Josephine said. "'Irm' is not grammatically correct. You mean to say, 'I have also finished my supper.'"

"Irm," Sunny insisted.

"My goodness, you do need grammar lessons," Aunt Josephine said. "All the more reason to go to the library. Come, children."

Leaving behind their half-full soup bowls, the Baudelaires followed Aunt Josephine down the hallway, taking care not to touch any of the doorknobs they passed. At the end of the hallway,

Aunt Josephine stopped and opened an ordinary-looking door, but when the children stepped through the door they arrived in a room that was anything but ordinary.

The library was neither square nor rectangular, like most rooms, but curved in the shape of an oval. One wall of the oval was devoted to books—rows and rows and rows of them, and every single one of them was about grammar. There was an encyclopedia of nouns placed in a series of simple wooden bookshelves, curved to fit the wall. There were very thick books on the history of verbs, lined up in metal bookshelves that were polished to a bright shine. And there were cabinets made of glass, with adjective manuals placed inside them as if they were for sale in a store instead of in someone's house. In the middle of the room were some comfortable-looking chairs, each with its own footstool so one could stretch out one's legs while reading.

But it was the other wall of the oval, at the

far end of the room, that drew the children's attention. From floor to ceiling, the wall was a window, just one enormous curved pane of glass, and beyond the glass was a spectacular view of Lake Lachrymose. When the children stepped forward to take a closer look, they felt as if they were flying high above the dark lake instead of merely looking out on it.

"This is the only way I can stand to look at the lake," Aunt Josephine said in a quiet voice. "From far away. If I get much closer I remember my last picnic on the beach with my darling Ike. I warned him to wait an hour after eating before he went into the lake, but he only waited forty-five minutes. He thought that was enough."

"Did he get cramps?" Klaus asked. "That's what's supposed to happen if you don't wait an hour before you swim."

"That's one reason," Aunt Josephine said, "but in Lake Lachrymose, there's another one. If you don't wait an hour after eating, the

Lachrymose Leeches will smell food on you, and attack."

"Leeches?" Violet asked.

"Leeches," Klaus explained, "are a bit like worms. They are blind and live in bodies of water, and in order to feed, they attach themselves to you and suck your blood."

Violet shuddered. "How horrible."

"Swoh!" Sunny shrieked, which probably meant something along the lines of "Why in the world would you go swimming in a lake full of leeches?"

"The Lachrymose Leeches," Aunt Josephine said, "are quite different from regular leeches. They each have six rows of very sharp teeth, and one very sharp nose—they can smell even the smallest bit of food from far, far away. The Lachrymose Leeches are usually quite harmless, preying only on small fish. But if they smell food on a human they will swarm around him and—and . . ." Tears came to Aunt Josephine's eyes, and she took out a pale pink handkerchief and dabbed them away. "I apologize, children. It is not grammatically correct to end a sentence with the word 'and', but I get so upset when I think about Ike that I cannot talk about his death."

"We're sorry we brought it up," Klaus said quickly. "We didn't mean to upset you."

"That's all right," Aunt Josephine said, blowing her nose. "It's just that I prefer to think of Ike in other ways. Ike always loved the sunshine, and I like to imagine that wherever he is now, it's as sunny as can be. Of course, nobody knows what happens to you after you die, but it's nice to think of my husband someplace very, very hot, don't you think?"

"Yes I do," Violet said. "It is very nice." She swallowed. She wanted to say something else to Aunt Josephine, but when you have only known someone for a few hours it is difficult to know what they would like to hear. "Aunt Josephine," she said timidly, "have you thought of moving someplace else? Perhaps if you lived somewhere far from Lake Lachrymose, you might feel better."

"We'd go with you," Klaus piped up.

"Oh, I could never sell this house," Aunt Josephine said. "I'm terrified of realtors."

The three Baudelaire youngsters looked at one another surreptitiously, a word which here means "while Aunt Josephine wasn't looking." None of them had ever heard of a person who was frightened of realtors.

There are two kinds of fears: rational and irrational—or, in simpler terms, fears that make sense and fears that don't. For instance, the Baudelaire orphans have a fear of Count Olaf, which makes perfect sense, because he is an evil man who wants to destroy them. But if they were afraid of lemon meringue pie, this would be an irrational fear, because lemon meringue pie is delicious and has never hurt a soul. Being afraid of a monster under the bed is perfectly rational, because there may in fact be a monster under your bed at any time, ready to eat you all up, but a fear of realtors is an irrational fear. Realtors, as I'm sure you know, are people who assist in the buying and selling of houses. Besides occasionally wearing an ugly yellow coat, the worst a realtor can do to you is show you a house that you find ugly, and so it is completely irrational to be terrified of them.

As Violet, Klaus, and Sunny looked down at the dark lake and thought about their new lives with Aunt Josephine, they experienced a fear themselves, and even a worldwide expert on fear would have difficulty saying whether this was a rational fear or an irrational fear. The Baudelaires' fear was that misfortune would soon befall them. On one hand, this was an irrational fear, because Aunt Josephine seemed like a good person, and Count Olaf was nowhere to be seen. But on the other hand, the Baudelaires had experienced so many terrible things that it seemed rational to think that another catastrophe was just around the corner.

There is a way of looking at life called "keeping things in perspective." This simply means "making yourself feel better by comparing the things that are happening to you right now against other things that have happened at a different time, or to different people." For instance, if you were upset about an ugly pimple on the end of your nose, you might try to feel better by keeping your pimple in perspective. You might compare your pimple situation to that of someone who was being eaten by a bear, and when you looked in the mirror at your ugly pimple, you could say to yourself, "Well, at least I'm not being eaten by a bear."

You can see at once why keeping things in perspective rarely works very well, because it is hard to concentrate on somebody else being eaten by a bear when you are staring at your own ugly pimple. So it was with the Baudelaire orphans in the days that followed. In the morning, when the children joined Aunt Josephine for a breakfast of orange juice and untoasted bread, Violet thought to herself, "Well, at least we're not being forced to cook for Count Olaf's disgusting theater troupe." In the afternoon, when Aunt Josephine would take them to the library and teach them all about grammar, Klaus thought to himself, "Well, at least Count Olaf isn't about to whisk us away to Peru." And in the evening, when the children joined Aunt Josephine for a dinner of orange juice and untoasted bread, Sunny thought to herself, "Zax!" which meant something along the lines of "Well, at least there isn't a sign of Count Olaf anywhere."

But no matter how much the three siblings compared their life with Aunt Josephine to the miserable things that had happened to them before, they couldn't help but be dissatisfied with their circumstances. In her free time, Violet would dismantle the gears and switches from the model train set, hoping to invent something that could prepare hot food without frightening Aunt Josephine, but she couldn't help wishing that Aunt Josephine would simply turn on the stove. Klaus would sit in one of the chairs in the library with his feet on a footstool, reading about grammar until the sun went down, but when he looked out at the gloomy lake he couldn't help wishing that they were still living with Uncle Monty and all of his reptiles. And Sunny would take time out from her schedule and bite the head of Pretty Penny, but she couldn't help wishing that their parents were still alive and that she and her siblings were safe and sound in the Baudelaire home.

Aunt Josephine did not like to leave the house very much, because there were so many things outside that frightened her, but one day the children told her what the cabdriver had said about Hurricane Herman approaching, and she agreed to take them into town in order to buy groceries. Aunt Josephine was afraid to drive in automobiles, because the doors might get stuck, leaving her trapped inside, so they walked the long way down the hill. By the time the Baudelaires reached the market their legs were sore from the walk.

"Are you sure that you won't let us cook for you?" Violet asked, as Aunt Josephine reached into the barrel of limes. "When we lived with Count Olaf, we learned how to make puttanesca sauce. It was quite easy and perfectly safe."

Aunt Josephine shook her head. "It is my responsibility as your caretaker to cook for you, and I am eager to try this recipe for cold lime stew. Count Olaf certainly does sound evil. Imagine forcing children to stand near a stove!"

"He was very cruel to us," Klaus agreed, not adding that being forced to cook had been the least of their problems when they lived with Count Olaf. "Sometimes I still have nightmares about the terrible tattoo on his ankle. It always scared me."

Aunt Josephine frowned, and patted her bun. "I'm afraid you made a grammatical mistake, Klaus," she said sternly. "When you said, 'It always scared me,' you sounded as if you meant that his ankle always scared you, but you meant his tattoo. So you should have said, 'The tattoo always scared me.' Do you understand?"

"Yes, I understand," Klaus said, sighing. "Thank you for pointing that out, Aunt Josephine."

"Niku!" Sunny shrieked, which probably meant something like "It wasn't very nice to point out Klaus's grammatical mistake when he was talking about something that upset him."

"No, no, Sunny," Aunt Josephine said firmly, looking up from her shopping list. "'Niku' isn't a word. Remember what we said about using correct English. Now, Violet, would you please get some cucumbers? I thought I would make chilled cucumber soup again sometime next week."

Violet groaned inwardly, a phrase which here means "said nothing but felt disappointed at the prospect of another chilly dinner," but she smiled at Aunt Josephine and headed down an aisle of the market in search of cucumbers. She looked wistfully at all the delicious food on the shelves that required turning on the stove in order to prepare it. Violet hoped that someday she could cook a nice hot meal for Aunt Josephine and her siblings using the invention she was working on with the model train engine. For a few moments she was so lost in her inventing thoughts that she didn't look where she was going until she walked right into someone.

"Excuse m—" Violet started to say, but when

she looked up she couldn't finish her sentence.
There stood a tall, thin man with a blue sailor
hat on his head and a black eye patch covering
his left eye. He was smiling eagerly down at
her as if she were a brightly wrapped birthday
present that he couldn't wait to rip open. His
fingers were long and bony, and he was leaning awkwardly to one side, a bit like Aunt
Josephine's house dangling over the hill. When
Violet looked down, she saw why: There was a
thick stump of wood where his left leg should
have been, and like most people with peg legs,
this man was leaning on his good leg, which
caused him to tilt. But even though Violet had
never seen anyone with a peg leg before, this
was not why she couldn't finish her sentence.
The reason why had to do with something
she *had* seen before—the bright, bright shine in
the man's one eye, and above it, just one long
eyebrow.

When someone is in disguise, and the disguise is not very good, one can describe it as a

transparent disguise. This does not mean that the person is wearing plastic wrap or glass or anything else transparent. It merely means that people can see through his disguise—that is, the disguise doesn't fool them for a minute. Violet wasn't fooled for even a second as she stood staring at the man she'd walked into. She knew at once it was Count Olaf.

"Violet, what are you doing in this aisle?" Aunt Josephine said, walking up behind her. "This aisle contains food that needs to be heated, and you know—" When she saw Count Olaf she stopped speaking, and for a second Violet thought that Aunt Josephine had recognized him, too. But then Aunt Josephine smiled, and Violet's hopes were dashed, a word which here means "shattered."

"Hello," Count Olaf said, smiling at Aunt Josephine. "I was just apologizing for running into your sister here."

Aunt Josephine's face grew bright red, seeming even brighter under her white hair. "Oh, no," she said, as Klaus and Sunny came down the aisle to see what all the fuss was about. "Violet is not my sister, sir. I am her legal guardian."

Count Olaf clapped one hand to his face as if Aunt Josephine had just told him she was the tooth fairy. "I cannot believe it," he said. "Madam, you don't look nearly old enough to be anyone's guardian."

Aunt Josephine blushed again. "Well, sir, I have lived by the lake my whole life, and some people have told me that it keeps me looking youthful."

"I would be happy to have the acquaintance of a local personage," Count Olaf said, tipping his blue sailor hat and using a silly word which here means "person." "I am new to this town, and beginning a new business, so I am eager to make new acquaintances. Allow me to introduce myself."

"Klaus and I are happy to introduce you," Violet said, with more bravery than I would have had when faced with meeting Count Olaf again. "Aunt Josephine, this is Count—"

"No, no, Violet," Aunt Josephine interrupted. "Watch your grammar. You should have said 'Klaus and I *will be* happy to introduce you,' because you haven't introduced us yet."

"But—" Violet started to say.

"Now, Veronica," Count Olaf said, his one eye shining brightly as he looked down at her. "Your guardian is right. And before you make any other mistakes, allow me to introduce myself. My name is Captain Sham, and I have a new business renting sailboats out on Damocles Dock. I am happy to make your acquaintance, Miss—?"

"I am Josephine Anwhistle," Aunt Josephine said. "And these are Violet, Klaus, and little Sunny Baudelaire."

"Little Sunny," Captain Sham repeated, sounding as if he were eating Sunny rather than greeting her. "It's a pleasure to meet all of you. Perhaps someday I can take you out on the lake for a little boat ride."

"Ging!" Sunny shrieked, which probably meant something like "I would rather eat dirt."

"We're not going anywhere with you," Klaus said.

Aunt Josephine blushed again, and looked sharply at the three children. "The children seem to have forgotten their manners as well as their grammar," she said. "Please apologize to Captain Sham at once."

"He's not Captain Sham," Violet said impatiently. "He's Count Olaf."

Aunt Josephine gasped, and looked from the anxious faces of the Baudelaires to the calm face of Captain Sham. He had a grin on his face, but his smile had slipped a notch, a phrase which here means "grown less confident as he waited to see if Aunt Josephine realized he was really Count Olaf in disguise."

Aunt Josephine looked him over from head to toe, and then frowned. "Mr. Poe told me to be on the watch for Count Olaf," she said finally, "but he did also say that you children tended to see him everywhere."

"We see him everywhere," Klaus said tiredly, "because he *is* everywhere."

"Who is this Count Omar person?" Captain Sham asked.

"Count *Olaf*," Aunt Josephine said, "is a terrible man who—"

"—is standing right in front of us," Violet finished. "I don't care what he calls himself. He has the same shiny eyes, the same single eyebrow—"

"But plenty of people have those characteristics," Aunt Josephine said. "Why, my mother-in-law had not only one eyebrow, but also only one ear."

"The tattoo!" Klaus said. "Look for the tattoo! Count Olaf has a tattoo of an eye on his left ankle."

Captain Sham sighed, and, with difficulty, lifted his peg leg so everyone could get a clear look at it. It was made of dark wood that was polished to shine as brightly as his eye, and attached to his left knee with a curved metal hinge. "But I don't even have a left ankle," he said, in a whiny voice. "It was all chewed away by the Lachrymose Leeches."

Aunt Josephine's eyes welled up, and she placed a hand on Captain Sham's shoulder. "Oh, you poor man," she said, and the children knew at once that they were doomed. "Did you hear what Captain Sham said?" she asked them.

Violet tried one more time, knowing it would probably be futile, a word which here means "filled with futility." "He's not Captain Sham," she said. "He's—"

"You don't think he would allow the Lachrymose Leeches to chew off his leg," Aunt Josephine said, "just to play a prank on you? Tell us, Captain Sham. Tell us how it happened."

"Well, I was sitting on my boat, just a few weeks ago," Captain Sham said. "I was eating some pasta with puttanesca sauce, and I spilled some on my leg. Before I knew it, the leeches were attacking."

"That's just how it happened with my husband," Aunt Josephine said, biting her lip. The Baudelaires, all three of them, clenched their fists in frustration. They knew that Captain Sham's story about the puttanesca sauce was as phony as his name, but they couldn't prove it.

"Here," Captain Sham said, pulling a small card out of his pocket and handing it to Aunt Josephine. "Take my business card, and next time you're in town perhaps we could enjoy a cup of tea."

"That sounds delightful," Aunt Josephine said, reading his card. "'Captain Sham's Sailboats. Every boat has it's own sail.' Oh, Captain, you have made a very serious grammatical error here."

"What?" Captain Sham said, raising his eyebrow.

"This card says 'it's,' with an apostrophe. I-T-apostrophe-S always means 'it is.' You don't mean to say 'Every boat has it is own sail.' You mean simply I-T-S, 'belonging to it.' It's a very common mistake, Captain Sham, but a dreadful one."

Captain Sham's face darkened, and it looked for a minute like he was going to raise his peg leg again and kick Aunt Josephine with all his might. But then he smiled and his face cleared. "Thank you for pointing that out," he said finally.

"You're welcome," Aunt Josephine said. "Come, children, it's time to pay for our groceries. I hope to see you soon, Captain Sham."

Captain Sham smiled and waved good-bye, but the Baudelaires watched as his smile turned to a sneer as soon as Aunt Josephine had turned her back. He had fooled her, and there was nothing the Baudelaires could do about it. They spent the rest of the afternoon trudging back up the hill carrying their groceries, but the heaviness of cucumbers and limes was nothing compared to the heaviness in the orphans' hearts. All the way up the hill, Aunt Josephine talked about Captain Sham and what a nice man he was and how much she hoped they would see him again, while the children knew he was really Count Olaf and a terrible man and hoped they would never see him for the rest of their lives.

There is an expression that, I am sad to say, is appropriate for this part of the story. The expression is "falling for something hook, line, and sinker," and it comes from the world of fishing. The hook, the line, and the sinker are all parts of a fishing rod, and they work together to lure fish out of the ocean to their doom. If somebody is falling for something hook, line, and sinker, they are believing a bunch of lies and may find themselves doomed as a result. Aunt Josephine was falling for Captain Sham's lies hook, line, and sinker, but it was Violet, Klaus, and Sunny who were feeling doomed. As they walked up the hill in silence, the children looked down at Lake Lachrymose and felt the chill of doom fall over their hearts. It made the three siblings feel cold and lost, as if they were not simply looking at the shadowy lake, but had been dropped into the middle of its depths.

Four

That night, the Baudelaire children sat at the table with Aunt Josephine and ate their dinner with a cold pit in their stomachs. Half of the pit came from the chilled lime stew that Aunt Josephine had prepared. But the other half—if not more than half—came from the knowledge that Count Olaf was in their lives once again.

"That Captain Sham is certainly a charming person," Aunt Josephine said, putting a piece of lime rind in her mouth. "He must be very lonely, moving to a new town and losing a leg. Maybe we could have him over for dinner."

"We keep trying to tell you, Aunt Josephine," Violet said, pushing the stew around on her plate so it would look like she'd eaten more than she actually had. "He's not Captain Sham. He's Count Olaf in disguise."

"I've had enough of this nonsense," Aunt Josephine said. "Mr. Poe told me that Count Olaf had a tattoo on his left ankle and one eyebrow over his eyes. Captain Sham doesn't have a left ankle and only has one eye. I can't believe you would dare to disagree with a man who has eye problems."

"I have eye problems," Klaus said, pointing to his glasses, "and you're disagreeing with me."

"I will thank you not to be impertinent," Aunt Josephine said, using a word which here means "pointing out that I'm wrong, which annoys me." "It is very annoying. You will have to accept, once and for all, that Captain Sham is *not* Count Olaf." She reached into her pocket and pulled out the business card. "Look at his card. Does it say Count Olaf? No. It says Captain Sham. The card does have a serious grammatical error on it, but it is nevertheless proof that Captain Sham is who he says he is."

Aunt Josephine put the business card down on the dinner table, and the Baudelaires looked at it and sighed. Business cards, of course, are not proof of anything. Anyone can go to a print shop and have cards made that say anything they like. The king of Denmark can order business cards that say he sells golf balls. Your dentist can order business cards that say she is your grandmother. In order to escape from the castle of an enemy of mine, I once had cards printed that said I was an admiral in the French navy. Just because something is typed—whether it is typed on a business card or typed in a newspaper or book—this does not mean that it is true. The three siblings were well aware of this simple fact but could not find the words to convince Aunt Josephine. So they merely looked at Aunt Josephine, sighed, and silently pretended to eat their stew.

It was so quiet in the dining room that everyone jumped—Violet, Klaus, Sunny, and even Aunt Josephine—when the telephone rang. "My goodness!" Aunt Josephine said. "What should we do?"

"Minka!" Sunny shrieked, which probably meant something like "Answer it, of course!"

Aunt Josephine stood up from the table, but didn't move even as the phone rang a second time. "It might be important," she said, "but I don't know if it's worth the risk of electrocution."

"If it makes you feel more comfortable," Violet said, wiping her mouth with her napkin, "I will answer the phone." Violet stood up and walked to the phone in time to answer it on the third ring.

"Hello?" she asked.

"Is this Mrs. Anwhistle?" a wheezy voice asked.

"No," Violet replied. "This is Violet Baude-laire. May I help you?"

"Put the old woman on the phone, orphan," the voice said, and Violet froze, realizing it was Captain Sham. Quickly, she stole a glance at Aunt Josephine, who was now watching Violet nervously.

"I'm sorry," Violet said into the phone. "You must have the wrong number."

"Don't play with me, you wretched girl—" Captain Sham started to say, but Violet hung up the phone, her heart pounding, and turned to Aunt Josephine.

"Someone was asking for the Hopalong Dancing School," she said, lying quickly. "I told them they had the wrong number."

"What a brave girl you are," Aunt Josephine murmured. "Picking up the phone like that."

"It's actually very safe," Violet said.

"Haven't you ever answered the phone, Aunt Josephine?" Klaus asked.

"Ike almost always answered it," Aunt

Josephine said, "and he used a special glove for safety. But now that I've seen you answer it, maybe I'll give it a try next time somebody calls."

The phone rang, and Aunt Josephine jumped again. "Goodness," she said, "I didn't think it would ring again so soon. What an adventurous evening!"

Violet stared at the phone, knowing it was Captain Sham calling back. "Would you like me to answer it again?" she asked.

"No, no," Aunt Josephine said, walking toward the small ringing phone as if it were a big barking dog. "I said I'd try it, and I will." She took a deep breath, reached out a nervous hand, and picked up the phone.

"Hello?" she said. "Yes, this is she. Oh, hello, Captain Sham. How lovely to hear your voice." Aunt Josephine listened for a moment, and then blushed bright red. "Well, that's very nice of you to say, Captain Sham, but—what? Oh, all right. That's very nice of you to say, *Julio*. What?

What? Oh, what a lovely idea. But please hold on one moment."

Aunt Josephine held a hand over the receiver and faced the three children. "Violet, Klaus, Sunny, please go to your room," she said. "Captain Sham—I mean Julio, he asked me to call him by his first name—is planning a surprise for you children, and he wants to discuss it with me."

"We don't want a surprise," Klaus said.

"Of course you do," Aunt Josephine said. "Now run along so I can discuss it without your eavesdropping."

"We're not eavesdropping," Violet said, "but I think it would be better if we stayed here."

"Perhaps you are confused about the meaning of the word 'eavesdropping,'" Aunt Josephine said. "It means 'listening in.' If you stay here, you will be eavesdropping. Please go to your room."

"We *know* what eavesdropping means," Klaus said, but he followed his sisters down the hallway to their room. Once inside, they looked at one another in silent frustration. Violet put aside pieces of the toy caboose that she had planned to examine that evening to make room on her bed for the three of them to lie beside one another and frown at the ceiling.

"I thought we'd be safe here," Violet said glumly. "I thought that anybody who was frightened of realtors would never be friendly to Count Olaf, no matter how he was disguised."

"Do you think that he actually let leeches chew off his leg," Klaus wondered, shuddering, "just to hide his tattoo?"

"Choin!" Sunny shrieked, which probably meant "That seems a little drastic, even for Count Olaf."

"I agree with Sunny," Violet said. "I think he told that tale about leeches just to make Aunt Josephine feel sorry for him."

"And it sure worked," Klaus said, sighing. "After he told her that sob story, she fell for his disguise hook, line, and sinker."

"At least she isn't as trusting as Uncle Monty," Violet pointed out. "He let Count Olaf move right into the house."

"At least then we could keep an eye on him," Klaus replied.

"Ober!" Sunny remarked, which meant something along the lines of "Although we still didn't save Uncle Monty."

"What do you think he's up to this time?" Violet asked. "Maybe he plans to take us out in one of his boats and drown us in the lake."

"Maybe he wants to push this whole house off the mountain," Klaus said, "and blame it on Hurricane Herman."

"Haftu!" Sunny said glumly, which probably meant something like "Maybe he wants to put the Lachrymose Leeches in our beds."

"Maybe, maybe, maybe," Violet said. "All these maybes won't get us anywhere."

"We could call Mr. Poe and tell him Count

Olaf is here," Klaus said. "Maybe he could come and fetch us."

"That's the biggest maybe of them all," Violet said. "It's always impossible to convince Mr. Poe of anything, and Aunt Josephine docsn't believe us even though she saw Count Olaf with her own eyes."

"She doesn't even think she saw Count Olaf," Klaus agreed sadly. "She thinks she saw *Captain Sham.*"

Sunny nibbled halfheartedly on Pretty Penny's head and muttered "Poch!" which probably meant "You mean *Julio.*"

"Then I don't see what we can do," Klaus said, "except keep our eyes and ears open."

"Doma," Sunny agreed.

"You're both right," Violet said. "We'll just have to keep a very careful watch."

The Baudelaire orphans nodded solemnly, but the cold pit in their stomachs had not gone away. They all felt that keeping watch wasn't really much of a plan for defending themselves from Captain Sham, and as it grew later and later it worried them more and more. Violet tied her hair up in a ribbon to keep it out of her eyes, as if she were inventing something, but she thought and thought for hours and hours and was unable to invent another plan. Klaus stared at the ceiling with the utmost concentration, as if something very interesting were written on it, but nothing helpful occurred to him as the hour grew later and later. And Sunny bit Pretty Penny's head over and over, but no matter how long she bit it she couldn't think of anything to ease the Baudelaires' worries.

I have a friend named Gina-Sue who is socialist, and Gina-Sue has a favorite saying: "You can't lock up the barn after the horses are gone." It means simply that sometimes even the best of plans will occur to you when it is too late. This, I'm sorry to say, is the case with the Baudelaire orphans and their plan to keep a close watch on Captain Sham, for after hours and hours of worrying they heard an enormous crash of shattering glass, and knew at once that keeping watch hadn't been a good enough plan.

"What was that noise?" Violet said, getting up off the bed.

"It sounded like breaking glass," Klaus said worriedly, walking toward the bedroom door.

"Vestu!" Sunny shrieked, but her siblings did not have time to figure out what she meant as they all hurried down the hallway.

"Aunt Josephine! Aunt Josephine!" Violet called, but there was no answer. She peered up and down the hallway, but everything was quiet. "Aunt Josephine!" she called again. Violet led the way as the three orphans ran into the dining room, but their guardian wasn't there either. The candles on the table were still lit, casting a flickering glow on the business card and the bowls of cold lime stew.

"Aunt Josephine!" Violet called again, and

the children ran back out to the hallway and toward the door of the library. As she ran, Violet couldn't help but remember how she and her siblings had called Uncle Monty's name, early one morning, just before discovering the tragedy that had befallen him. "Aunt Josephine!" she called. "Aunt Josephine!" She couldn't help but remember all the times she had woken up in the middle of the night, calling out the names of her parents as she dreamed, as she so often did, of the terrible fire that had claimed their lives. "Aunt Josephine!" she said, reaching the library door. Violet was afraid that she was calling out Aunt Josephine's name when her aunt could no longer hear it.

"Look," Klaus said, and pointed to the door. A piece of paper, folded in half, was attached to the wood with a thumbtack. Klaus pried the paper loose and unfolded it.

"What is it?" Violet asked, and Sunny craned her little neck to see.

"It's a note," Klaus said, and read it out loud:

Violet, Klaus, and Sunny—
By the time you read this note, my life will be at
it's end. My heart is as cold as Ike and I find
life inbearable. I know your children may not
understand the sad life of a dowadger, or
what would have leaded me to this desperate akt,
but please know that I am much happier this
way. As my last will and testament, I leave you
three in the care of Captain Sham, a kind and
honorable men. Please think of me kindly even
though I'd done this terrible thing.
—Your Aunt Josephine

"Oh no," Klaus said quietly when he was finished reading. He turned the piece of paper over and over as if he had read it incorrectly, as if it said something different. "Oh no," he said again, so faintly that it was as if he didn't even know he was speaking out loud.

Without a word Violet opened the door to the library, and the Baudelaires took a step inside and found themselves shivering. The room was freezing cold, and after one glance the orphans knew why. The Wide Window had shattered. Except for a few shards that still stuck to the window frame, the enormous pane of glass was gone, leaving a vacant hole that looked out into the still blackness of the night.

The cold night air rushed through the hole, rattling the bookshelves and making the children shiver up against one another, but despite the cold the orphans walked carefully to the empty space where the window had been, and looked down. The night was so black that it seemed as if there was absolutely nothing beyond the window. Violet, Klaus, and Sunny stood there for a moment and remembered the fear they had felt, just a few days ago, when they were standing in this very same spot. They knew now that their fear had been rational.

Huddling together, looking down into the blackness, the Baudelaires knew that their plan to keep a careful watch had come too late. They had locked the barn door, but poor Aunt Josephine was already gone.

Violet, Klaus, and Sunny—
By the time you read this note,
my life will be at it's end. My heart
is as cold as Ike and I find life
inbearable. I know your
children may not
understand the sad
life of a dowadger, or
what would have leaded
me to this desperate akt, but
please know that I am much

happier this way. As my last will and testament,
I leave you three in the care of Captain Sham, a
kind and honorable men. Please think of me
kindly even though I'd done this terrible thing.
——Your Aunt Josephine

"*Stop it!*" Violet cried. "Stop reading it out loud, Klaus! We already know what it says."

"I just can't believe it," Klaus said, turning the paper around for the umpteenth time. The Baudelaire orphans were sitting glumly around the dining-room table with the cold lime stew in bowls and dread in their hearts. Violet had called Mr. Poe and told him what had happened, and the Baudelaires, too anxious to sleep, had stayed up the whole night waiting for him to arrive on the first Fickle Ferry of the day. The candles were almost completely burned down, and Klaus had to lean forward to read Josephine's note. "There's something funny about this note, but I can't put my finger on it."

"How can you say such a thing?" Violet asked. "Aunt Josephine has thrown herself out of the window. There's nothing funny about it at all."

"Not funny as in a funny joke," Klaus said. "Funny as in a funny smell. Why, in the very first sentence she says 'my life will be at it's end.'"

"And now it is," Violet said, shuddering.

"That's not what I mean," Klaus said impatiently. "She uses it's, I-T-apostrophe-S, which always means 'it is.' But you wouldn't say 'my life will be at it is end.' She means I-T-S, 'belonging to it.'" He picked up Captain Sham's business card, which was still lying on the table. "Remember when she saw this card? 'Every boat has it's own sail.' She said it was a serious grammatical error."

"Who cares about grammatical errors," Violet asked, "when Aunt Josephine has jumped out the window?"

"But Aunt Josephine would have cared,"

Klaus pointed out. "That's what she cared about most: grammar. Remember, she said it was the greatest joy in life."

"Well, it wasn't enough," Violet said sadly. "No matter how much she liked grammar, it says she found her life unbearable."

"But that's another error in the note," Klaus said. "It doesn't say *un*bearable, with a U. It says *in*bearable, with an I."

"*You* are being unbearable, with a U," Violet cried.

"And *you* are being stupid, with an S," Klaus snapped.

"Aget!" Sunny shrieked, which meant something along the lines of "Please stop fighting!" Violet and Klaus looked at their baby sister and then at one another. Oftentimes, when people are miserable, they will want to make other people miserable, too. But it never helps.

"I'm sorry, Klaus," Violet said meekly. "You're not unbearable. Our situation is unbearable."

"I know," Klaus said miserably. "I'm sorry,

too. You're not stupid, Violet. You're very clever. In fact, I hope you're clever enough to get us out of this situation. Aunt Josephine has jumped out the window and left us in the care of Captain Sham, and I don't know what we can do about it."

"Well, Mr. Poe is on his way," Violet said. "He said on the phone that he would be here first thing in the morning, so we don't have long to wait. Maybe Mr. Poe can be of some help."

"I guess so," Klaus said, but he and his sisters looked at one another and sighed. They knew that the chances of Mr. Poe being of much help were rather slim. When the Baudelaires lived with Count Olaf, Mr. Poe was not helpful when the children told him about Count Olaf's cruelty. When the Baudelaires lived with Uncle Monty, Mr. Poe was not helpful when the children told him about Count Olaf's treachery. It seemed clear that Mr. Poe would not be of any help in this situation, either.

One of the candles burned out in a small

puff of smoke, and the children sank down lower in their chairs. You probably know of a plant called the Venus flytrap, which grows in the tropics. The top of the plant is shaped like an open mouth, with toothlike spines around the edges. When a fly, attracted by the smell of the flower, lands on the Venus flytrap, the mouth of the plant begins to close, trapping the fly. The terrified fly buzzes around the closed mouth of the plant, but there is nothing it can do, and the plant slowly, slowly, dissolves the fly into nothing. As the darkness of the house closed in around them, the Baudelaire youngsters felt like the fly in this situation. It was as if the disastrous fire that took the lives of their parents had been the beginning of a trap, and they hadn't even known it. They buzzed from place to place—Count Olaf's house in the city, Uncle Monty's home in the country, and now, Aunt Josephine's house overlooking the lake—but their own misfortune always closed

around them, tighter and tighter, and it seemed
to the three siblings that before too long they
would dissolve away to nothing.

"We could rip up the note," Klaus said finally.
"Then Mr. Poe wouldn't know about Aunt
Josephine's wishes, and we wouldn't end up
with Captain Sham."

"But I already told Mr. Poe that Aunt
Josephine left a note," Violet said.

"Well, we could do a forgery," Klaus said,
using a word which here means "write something yourself and pretend somebody else wrote
it." "We'll write everything she wrote, but we'll
leave out the part about Captain Sham."

"Aha!" Sunny shrieked. This word was a
favorite of Sunny's, and unlike most of her
words, it needed no translation. What Sunny
meant was "Aha!", an expression of discovery.

"Of course!" Violet cried. "That's what
Captain Sham did! *He* wrote this letter, not Aunt
Josephine!"

Behind his glasses, Klaus's eyes lit up. "That explains *it's*!"

"That explains *inbearable*!" Violet said.

"Leep!" Sunny shrieked, which probably meant "Captain Sham threw Aunt Josephine out the window and then wrote this note to hide his crime."

"What a terrible thing to do," Klaus said, shuddering as he thought of Aunt Josephine falling into the lake she feared so much.

"Imagine the terrible things he will do to us," Violet said, "if we don't expose his crime. I can't wait until Mr. Poe gets here so we can tell him what happened."

With perfect timing, the doorbell rang, and the Baudelaires hurried to answer it. Violet led her siblings down the hallway, looking wistfully at the radiator as she remembered how afraid of it Aunt Josephine was. Klaus followed closely behind, touching each doorknob gently in memory of Aunt Josephine's warnings about them shattering into pieces. And when they reached the door, Sunny looked mournfully at the welcome mat that Aunt Josephine thought could cause someone to break their neck. Aunt Josephine had been so careful to avoid anything that she thought might harm her, but harm had still come her way.

Violet opened the peeling white door, and there stood Mr. Poe in the gloomy light of dawn. "Mr. Poe," Violet said. She intended to tell him immediately of their forgery theory, but as soon as she saw him, standing in the doorway with a white handkerchief in one hand and a black briefcase in the other, her words stuck in her throat. Tears are curious things, for like earthquakes or puppet shows they can occur at any time, without any warning and without any good reason. "Mr. Poe," Violet said again, and without any warning she and her siblings burst into tears. Violet cried, her shoulders shaking with sobs, and Klaus cried, the tears making his glasses slip down his nose, and Sunny cried, her open mouth revealing her four teeth. Mr. Poe put down his briefcase and put away his hand-kerchief. He was not very good at comforting people, but he put his arms around the children the best he could, and murmured "There, there," which is a phrase some people murmur to comfort other people despite the fact that it doesn't really mean anything.

Mr. Poe couldn't think of anything else to say that might have comforted the Baudelaire orphans, but I wish now that I had the power to go back in time and speak to these three sobbing children. If I could, I could tell the Baudelaires that like earthquakes and puppet shows, their tears were occurring not only without warning but without good reason. The youngsters were crying, of course, because they thought Aunt Josephine was dead, and I wish I had the power to go back and tell them that they were wrong. But of course, I cannot. I am not on top of the hill, overlooking Lake Lachrymose, on that gloomy morning. I am sitting in my room, in the middle of the night, writing down this story and looking out my window at the graveyard behind my home. I cannot tell the Baudelaire orphans that they are wrong, but I can tell you, as the orphans cry in Mr. Poe's arms, that Aunt Josephine is not dead.

Not yet.

Chapter Six

Mr. Poe frowned, sat down at the table, and took out his handkerchief. "Forgery?" he repeated. The Baudelaire orphans had shown him the shattered window in the library. They had shown him the note that had been thumb-tacked to the door. And they had shown him the business card with the grammatical mistake on it. "Forgery is a very serious charge," he said sternly, and blew his nose.

"Not as serious as murder," Klaus pointed out. "And that's what Captain Sham did. He murdered Aunt Josephine and forged a note."

"But why would this Captain Sham person,"

Mr. Poe asked, "go to all this trouble just to place you under his care?"

"We've already told you," Violet said, trying to hide her impatience. "Captain Sham is really Count Olaf in disguise."

"These are very serious accusations," Mr. Poe said firmly. "I understand that the three of you have had some terrible experiences, and I hope you're not letting your imagination get the best of you. Remember when you lived with Uncle Monty? You were convinced that his assistant, Stephano, was really Count Olaf in disguise."

"But Stephano *was* Count Olaf in disguise," Klaus exclaimed.

"That's not the point," Mr. Poe said. "The point is that you can't jump to conclusions. If you really think this note is a forgery, then we have to stop talking about disguises and do an investigation. Somewhere in this house, I'm sure we can find something that your Aunt Josephine has written. We can compare the handwriting and see if this note matches up."

The Baudelaire orphans looked at one another. "Of course," Klaus said. "If the note we found on the library door doesn't match Aunt Josephine's handwriting, then it was obviously written by somebody else. We didn't think of that."

Mr. Poe smiled. "You see? You are very intelligent children, but even the most intelligent people in the world often need the help of a banker. Now, where can we find a sample of Aunt Josephine's handwriting?"

"In the kitchen," Violet said promptly. "She left her shopping list in the kitchen when we got home from the market."

"Chuni!" Sunny shrieked, which probably meant "Let's go to the kitchen and get it," and that's exactly what they did. Aunt Josephine's kitchen was very small and had a large white sheet covering the stove and the oven—for safety, Aunt Josephine had explained, during her tour. There was a countertop where she prepared the food, a refrigerator where she stored the food, and a sink where she washed away the food nobody had eaten. To one side of the countertop was a small piece of paper on which Aunt Josephine had made her list, and Violet crossed the kitchen to retrieve it. Mr. Poe turned on the lights, and Violet held the shopping list up to the note to see if they matched.

There are men and women who are experts in the field of handwriting analysis. They are called graphologists, and they attend graphological schools in order to get their degree in graphology. You might think that this situation would call for a graphologist, but there are times when an expert's opinion is unnecessary. For instance, if a friend of yours brought you her pet dog, and said she was concerned because it wasn't laying eggs, you would not have to be a veterinarian to tell her that dogs do not lay eggs and so there was nothing to worry about.

Yes, there are some questions that are so simple that anyone can answer them, and Mr. Poe and the Baudelaire orphans instantly knew the answer to the question "Does the handwriting on the shopping list match the handwriting on the note?" The answer was yes. When Aunt Josephine had written "Vinegar" on the shopping list, she had curved the tips of the V into tiny spirals—the same spirals that decorated the tips of the V in "Violet," on the note. When she had written "Cucumbers" on the shopping list, the Cs were slightly squiggly, like earthworms, and the same earthworms appeared in the words "cold" and "Captain Sham" on the note. When Aunt Josephine had written "Limes" on the shopping list, the *i* was dotted with an oval rather than a circle, just as it was in "my life will be at it's end." There was no doubt that Aunt Josephine had written on both the pieces of paper that Mr. Poe and the Baudelaires were examining.

"I don't think there's any doubt that Aunt Josephine wrote on both these pieces of paper," Mr. Poe said.

"But—" Violet began.

"There are no buts about it," Mr. Poe said. "Look at the curvy V's. Look at the squiggly C's. Look at the oval dots over the I's. I'm no graphologist, but I can certainly tell that these were written by the same person."

"You're right," Klaus said miserably. "I know that Captain Sham is behind this somehow, but Aunt Josephine definitely wrote this note."

"And that," Mr. Poe said, "makes it a legal document."

"Does that mean we have to live with Captain Sham?" Violet asked, her heart sinking.

"I'm afraid so," Mr. Poe replied. "Someone's last will and testament is an official statement of the wishes of the deceased. You were placed in Aunt Josephine's care, so she had the right to assign you to a new caretaker before she leaped out the window. It is very shocking, certainly, but it is entirely legal."

"We won't go live with him," Klaus said fiercely. "He's the worst person on earth."

"He'll do something terrible, I know it,"

Violet said. "All he's after is the Baudelaire fortune."

"Gind!" Sunny shrieked, which meant something like "Please don't make us live with this evil man."

"I know you don't like this Captain Sham person," Mr. Poe said, "but there's not much I can do about it. I'm afraid the law says that that's where you'll go."

"We'll run away," Klaus said.

"You will do nothing of the kind," Mr. Poe said sternly. "Your parents entrusted me to see that you would be cared for properly. You want to honor your parents' wishes, don't you?"

"Well, yes," Violet said, "but—"

"Then please don't make a fuss," Mr. Poe said. "Think of what your poor mother and father would say if they knew you were threatening to run away from your guardian."

The Baudelaire parents, of course, would have been horrified to learn that their children were to be in the care of Captain Sham, but before the children could say this to Mr. Poe, he had moved on to other matters. "Now, I think the easiest thing to do would be to meet with Captain Sham and go over some details. Where is his business card? I'll phone him now."

"On the table, in the dining room," Klaus said glumly, and Mr. Poe left the kitchen to make the call. The Baudelaires looked at Aunt Josephine's shopping list and the suicide note.

"I just can't believe it," Violet said. "I was sure we were on the right track with the forgery idea."

"Me too," Klaus said. "Captain Sham has done something here—I *know* he has—but he's been even sneakier than usual."

"We'd better be smarter than usual, then," Violet replied, "because we've got to convince Mr. Poe before it's too late."

"Well, Mr. Poe said he had to go over some details," Klaus said. "Perhaps that will take a long time."

"I got ahold of Captain Sham," Mr. Poe said, coming back into the kitchen. "He was shocked to hear of Aunt Josephine's death but overjoyed at the prospect of raising you children. We're meeting him in a half hour for lunch at a restaurant in town, and after lunch we'll go over the details of your adoption. By tonight you should be staying in his house. I'm sure you're relieved that this can be sorted out so quickly."

Violet and Sunny stared at Mr. Poe, too dismayed to speak. Klaus was silent too, but he was staring hard at something else. He was staring at Aunt Josephine's note. His eyes were focused in concentration behind his glasses as he stared and stared at it, without blinking. Mr. Poe took his white handkerchief out of his pocket and coughed into it at great length and with great gusto, a word which here means "in a way which produced a great deal of phlegm." But none of the Baudelaires said a word.

"Well," Mr. Poe said finally, "I will call for

a taxicab. There's no use walking down that enormous hill. You children comb your hair and put your coats on. It's very windy out and it's getting cold. I think a storm might be approaching."

Mr. Poe left to make his phone call, and the Baudelaires trudged to their room. Rather than comb their hair, however, Sunny and Violet immediately turned to Klaus. "What?" Violet asked him.

"*What* what?" Klaus answered.

"Don't give me that *what* what," Violet answered. "You've figured something out, that's *what* what. I know you have. You were rereading Aunt Josephine's note for the umpteenth time, but you had an expression as if you had just figured something out. Now, what is it?"

"I'm not sure," Klaus said, looking over the note one more time. "I might have begun figuring something out. Something that could help us. But I need more time."

"But we don't have any time!" Violet cried.

"We're going to have lunch with Captain Sham *right now*!"

"Then we're going to have to make some more time, somehow," Klaus said determinedly.

"Come on, children!" Mr. Poe called from the hallway. "The cab will be here any minute! Get your coats and let's go!"

Violet sighed, but went to the closet and took out all three Baudelaire coats. She handed Klaus his coat, and buttoned Sunny into her coat as she talked to her brother. "How can we make more time?" Violet asked.

"You're the inventor," Klaus answered, buttoning his coat.

"But you can't invent things like time," Violet said. "You can invent things like automatic popcorn poppers. You can invent things like steam-powered window washers. But you can't invent more *time*." Violet was so certain she couldn't invent more time that she didn't even put her hair up in a ribbon to keep it out of her eyes. She merely gave Klaus a look of frustration and confusion, and started to put on her coat. But as she did up the buttons she realized she didn't even need to put her hair up in a ribbon, because the answer was right there with her.

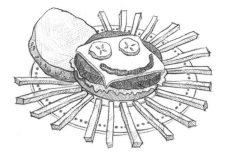

"*Hello*, I'm Larry, your waiter," said Larry, the Baudelaire orphans' waiter. He was a short, skinny man in a goofy clown costume with a name tag pinned to his chest that read LARRY. "Welcome to the Anxious Clown restaurant—where everybody has a good time, whether they like it or not. I can see we have a whole family lunching together today, so allow me to recommend the Extra Fun Special Family Appetizer. It's a bunch of things fried up together and served with a sauce."

"What a wonderful idea," Captain Sham said,

smiling in a way that showed all of his yellow teeth. "An Extra Fun Special Family Appetizer for an extra fun special family—*mine*."

"I'll just have water, thank you," Violet said.

"Same with me," Klaus said. "And a glass of ice cubes for my baby sister, please."

"I'll have a cup of coffee with nondairy creamer," Mr. Poe said.

"Oh, no, Mr. Poe," Captain Sham said. "Let's share a nice big bottle of red wine."

"No, thank you, Captain Sham," Mr. Poe said. "I don't like to drink during banking hours."

"But this is a celebratory lunch," Captain Sham exclaimed. "We should drink a toast to my three new children. It's not every day that a man becomes a father."

"Please, Captain," Mr. Poe said. "It is heartening to see that you are glad to raise the Baudelaires, but you must understand that the children are rather upset about their Aunt Josephine."

There is a lizard called the chameleon that, as you probably know, can change color instantly to blend into its surroundings. Besides being slimy and cold-blooded, Captain Sham resembled the chameleon in that he was chameleonic, a word means "able to blend in with any situation." Since Mr. Poe and the Baudelaires had arrived at the Anxious Clown, Captain Sham had been unable to conceal his excitement at having the children almost in his clutches. But now that Mr. Poe had pointed out that the occasion actually called for sadness, Captain Sham instantly began to speak in a mournful voice. "I am upset, too," he said, brushing a tear away from beneath his eyepatch. "Josephine was one of my oldest and dearest friends."

"You met her *yesterday*," Klaus said, "in the grocery store."

"It does only seem like yesterday," Captain Sham said, "but it was really years ago. She and I met in cooking school. We were oven partners in the Advanced Baking Course."

"You weren't *oven partners*," Violet said, disgusted at Captain Sham's lies. "Aunt Josephine was desperately afraid of turning on the oven. She never would have attended cooking school."

"We soon became friends," Captain Sham said, going on with his story as if no one had interrupted, "and one day she said to me, 'if I ever adopt some orphans and then meet an untimely death, promise me you will raise them for me.' I told her I would, but of course I never thought I would have to keep my promise."

"That's a very sad story," Larry said, and everyone turned to see that their waiter was still standing over them. "I didn't realize this was a sad occasion. In that case, allow me to recommend the Cheer-Up Cheeseburgers. The pickles, mustard, and ketchup make a little smiley face on top of the burger, which is guaranteed to get you smiling, too."

"That sounds like a good idea," Captain Sham said. "Bring us all Cheer-Up Cheeseburgers, Larry."

"They'll be here in a jiffy," the waiter promised, and at last he was gone.

"Yes, yes," Mr. Poe said, "but after we've finished our cheeseburgers, Captain Sham, there are some important papers for you to sign. I have them in my briefcase, and after lunch we'll look them over."

"And then the children will be mine?" Captain Sham asked.

"Well, you will be caring for them, yes," Mr. Poe said. "Of course, the Baudelaire fortune will still be under my supervision, until Violet comes of age."

"What fortune?" Captain Sham asked, his eyebrow curling. "I don't know anything about a fortune."

"Duna!" Sunny shrieked, which meant something along the lines of "Of course you do!"

"The Baudelaire parents," Mr. Poe explained, "left an enormous fortune behind, and the children inherit it when Violet comes of age."

"Well, I have no interest in a fortune,"

Captain Sham said. "I have my sailboats. I wouldn't touch a penny of it."

"Well, that's good," Mr. Poe said, "because you *can't* touch a penny of it."

"We'll see," Captain Sham said.

"What?" Mr. Poe asked.

"Here are your Cheer-Up Cheeseburgers!" Larry sang out, appearing at their table with a tray full of greasy-looking food. "Enjoy your meal."

Like most restaurants filled with neon lights and balloons, the Anxious Clown served terrible food. But the three orphans had not eaten all day, and had not eaten anything warm for a long time, so even though they were sad and anxious they found themselves with quite an appetite. After a few minutes without conversation, Mr. Poe began to tell a very dull story about something that had happened at the bank. Mr. Poe was so busy talking, Klaus and Sunny were so busy pretending to be interested, and Captain Sham was so busy wolfing down his meal, that nobody noticed what Violet was up to.

When Violet had put on her coat to go out into the wind and cold, she had felt the lump of something in her pocket. The lump was the bag of peppermints that Mr. Poe had given the Baudelaires the day they had arrived at Lake Lachrymose, and it had given her an idea. As Mr. Poe droned on and on, she carefully, carefully, took the bag of peppermints out of her coat pocket and opened it. To her dismay, they were the kind of peppermints that are each wrapped up in a little bit of cellophane. Placing her hands underneath the table, she unwrapped three peppermints, using the utmost—the word "utmost," when it is used here, means "most"— care not to make any of those crinkling noises that come from unwrapping candy and are so annoying in movie theaters. At last, she had three bare peppermints sitting on the napkin in her lap. Without drawing attention to herself, she put one on Klaus's lap and one on Sunny's.

When her younger siblings felt something appear in their laps and looked down and saw the peppermints, they at first thought the eldest Baudelaire orphan had lost her mind. But after a moment, they understood.

If you are allergic to a thing, it is best not to put that thing in your mouth, particularly if the thing is cats. But Violet, Klaus, and Sunny all knew that this was an emergency. They needed time alone to figure out Captain Sham's plan, and how to stop it, and although causing allergic reactions is a rather drastic way of getting time by yourself, it was the only thing they could think of. So while neither of the adults at the table were watching, all three children put the peppermints into their mouths and waited.

The Baudelaire allergies are famous for being quick-acting, so the orphans did not have long to wait. In a few minutes, Violet began to break out in red, itchy hives, Klaus's tongue started to swell up, and Sunny, who of course had never eaten a peppermint, broke out in hives *and* had her tongue swell up.

Mr. Poe finally finished telling his story and then noticed the orphans' condition. "Why, children," he said, "you look *terrible*! Violet, you have red patches on your skin. Klaus, your tongue is hanging out of your mouth. Sunny, both things are happening to you."

"There must be something in this food that we're allergic to," Violet said.

"My goodness," Mr. Poe said, watching a hive on Violet's arm grow to the size of a hard-boiled egg.

"Just take deep breaths," Captain Sham said, scarcely looking up from his cheeseburger.

"I feel terrible," Violet said, and Sunny began to wail. "I think we should go home and lie down, Mr. Poe."

"Just lean back in your seat," Captain Sham said sharply. "There's no reason to leave when we're in the middle of lunch."

"Why, Captain Sham," Mr. Poe said, "the

children are quite ill. Violet is right. Come now, I'll pay the bill and we'll take the children home."

"No, no," Violet said quickly. "We'll get a taxi. You two stay here and take care of all the details."

Captain Sham gave Violet a sharp look. "I wouldn't dream of leaving you all alone," he said in a dark voice.

"Well, there is a lot of paperwork to go over," Mr. Poe said. He glanced at his meal, and the Baudelaires could see he was not too eager to leave the restaurant and care for sick children. "We wouldn't be leaving them alone for long."

"Our allergies are fairly mild," Violet said truthfully, scratching at one of her hives. She stood up and led her swollen-tongued siblings toward the front door. "We'll just lie down for an hour or two while you have a relaxing lunch. When you have signed all the papers, Captain Sham, you can just come and retrieve us."

Captain Sham's one visible eye grew as shiny

as Violet had ever seen it. "I'll do that," he replied. "I'll come and retrieve you very, very soon."

"Good-bye, children," Mr. Poe said. "I hope you feel better soon. You know, Captain Sham, there is someone at my bank who has terrible allergies. Why, I remember one time . . ."

"Leaving so soon?" Larry asked the three children as they buttoned up their coats. Outside, the wind was blowing harder, and it had started to drizzle as Hurricane Herman got closer and closer to Lake Lachrymose. But even so, the three children were eager to leave the Anxious Clown, and not just because the garish restaurant—the word "garish" here means "filled with balloons, neon lights, and obnoxious waiters"—was filled with balloons, neon lights, and obnoxious waiters. The Baudelaires knew that they had invented just a little bit of time for themselves, and they had to use every second of it.

When someone's tongue swells up due to an allergic reaction, it is often difficult to understand what they are saying.

"Bluh bluh bluh bluh bluh," Klaus said, as the three children got out of the taxi and headed toward the peeling white door of Aunt Josephine's house.

"I don't understand what you're saying," Violet said, scratching at a hive on her neck that was the exact shape of the state of Minnesota.

"*Bluh bluh bluh bluh bluh,*" Klaus repeated, or perhaps he was saying something else; I haven't the faintest idea.

"Never mind, never mind," Violet said, opening the door and ushering her siblings inside. "Now you have the time that you need to figure out whatever it is that you're figuring out."

"Bluh bluh bluh," Klaus bluhed.

"I still can't understand you," Violet said. She took Sunny's coat off, and then her own, and dropped them both on the floor. Normally, of course, one should hang up one's coat on a hook or in a closet, but itchy hives are very irritating and tend to make one abandon such matters. "I'm going to assume, Klaus, that you said something in agreement. Now, unless you need us to help you, I'm going to give Sunny and myself a baking soda bath to help our hives."

"Bluh!" Sunny shrieked. She meant to shriek "Gans!" which meant something along the lines of "Good, because my hives are driving me crazy!"

"Bluh," Klaus said, nodding vigorously, and he began hurrying down the hallway. Klaus had not taken off his coat, but it wasn't because of his own irritating allergic condition. It was because he was going someplace cold.

When Klaus opened the door of the library, he was surprised at how much had changed. The wind from the approaching hurricane had blown away the last of the window, and the rain had soaked some of Aunt Josephine's comfortable chairs, leaving dark, spreading stains. A few books had fallen from their shelves and blown over to the window, where water had swollen them. There are few sights sadder than a ruined book, but Klaus had no time to be sad. He knew Captain Sham would come and retrieve the Baudelaires as soon as he could, so he had to get right to work. First he took Aunt Josephine's note out of his pocket and placed it on the table, weighing it down with books so it wouldn't blow away in the wind. Then he crossed quickly to the shelves and began to scan the spines of the books, looking for titles. He chose three: *Basic Rules of Grammar and Punctuation*, *Handbook for*

Advanced Apostrophe Use, and *The Correct Spelling of Every English Word That Ever, Ever Existed*. Each of the books was as thick as a watermelon, and Klaus staggered under the weight of carrying all three. With a loud *thump* he dropped them on the table. "Bluh bluh bluh, bluh bluh bluh bluh," he mumbled to himself, and found a pen and got to work.

A library is normally a very good place to work in the afternoon, but not if its window has been smashed and there is a hurricane approaching. The wind blew colder and colder, and it rained harder and harder, and the room became more and more unpleasant. But Klaus took no notice of this. He opened all of the books and took copious—the word "copious" here means "lots of"—notes, stopping every so often to draw a circle around some part of what Aunt Josephine had written. It began to thunder outside, and with each roll of thunder the entire house shook, but Klaus kept flipping pages and writing things down. Then, as lightning began to flash outside, he stopped, and stared at the note for a long time, frowning intently. Finally, he wrote two words at the bottom of Aunt Josephine's note, concentrating so hard as he did so that when Violet and Sunny entered the library and called out his name he nearly jumped out of his chair.

"Bluh surprised bluh!" he shrieked, his heart pounding and his tongue a bit less swollen.

"I'm sorry," Violet said. "I didn't mean to surprise you."

"Bluh bluh take a baking soda bluh?" he asked.

"No," Violet replied. "We couldn't take a baking soda bath. Aunt Josephine doesn't have any baking soda, because she never turns on the oven to bake. We just took a regular bath. But that doesn't matter, Klaus. What have *you* been doing, in this freezing room? Why have you drawn circles all over Aunt Josephine's note?"

"Bluhdying grammar," he replied, gesturing to the books.

"Bluh?" Sunny shrieked, which probably meant "gluh?" which meant something along the lines of "Why are you wasting valuable time studying grammar?"

"Bluhcause," Klaus explained impatiently, "I think bluh Josephine left us a message in bluh note."

"She was miserable, and she threw herself out the window," Violet said, shivering in the wind. "What other message could there be?"

"There are too many grammatical mistakes in the bluh," Klaus said. "Aunt Josephine loved grammar, and she'd never make that many mistakes unless she had a bluh reason. So that's what I've been doing bluh—counting up the grammatical mistakes."

"Bluh," Sunny said, which meant something along the lines of "Please continue, Klaus."

Klaus wiped a few raindrops off his glasses and looked down at his notes. "Well, we already know that bluh first sentence uses the wrong 'its.' I think that was to get our attention. But look at the second bluhtence. 'My heart is as cold as Ike and I find life inbearable.'"

"But the correct word is *un*bearable," Violet said. "You told us that already."

"Bluh I think there's more," Klaus said. "'My heart is as cold as Ike' doesn't sound right to me. Remember, Aunt Josephine told us bluh liked to think of her husband someplace very hot."

"That's true," Violet said, remembering. "She said it right here in this very room. She said Ike liked the sunshine and so she imagined him someplace sunny."

"So I think Aunt Bluhsephine meant 'cold as *ice*,'" Klaus said.

"Okay, so we have *ice* and *un*bearable. So far this doesn't mean anything to me," Violet said.

"Me neither," Klaus said. "But look at bluh next part. 'I know your children may not understand the sad life of a dowadger.' We don't have any children."

"That's true," Violet said. "I'm not planning to have children until I am considerably older."

"So why would Aunt Josephine say 'your children'? I think she meant '*you* children.' And I looked up 'dowadger' in *The Correct Spelling of Every English Word That Ever, Ever Existed.*"

"Why?" Violet asked. "You already know it's a fancy word for widow."

"It *is* a bluhncy word for widow," Klaus replied, "but it's spelled D-O-W-A-G-E-R. Aunt Josephine added an extra D."

"Cold as *ice*," Violet said, counting on her fingers, "*un*bearable, *you* children, and an extra D in dowager. That's not much of a message, Klaus."

"Let me finish," Klaus said. "I discovered even more grammbluhtical mistakes. When she wrote, 'or what would have leaded me to this desperate akt,' she meant 'what would have *led* me,' and the word 'act,' of course, is spelled with a C."

"Coik!" Sunny shrieked, which meant "Thinking about all this is making me dizzy!"

"Me too, Sunny," Violet said, lifting her sister

up so she could sit on the table. "But let him finish."

"There are just bluh more," Klaus said, holding up two fingers. "One, she calls Captain Sham 'a kind and honorable men,' when she should have said 'a kind and honorable *man*.' And in the last sentence, Aunt Josephine wrote 'Please think of me kindly even though I'd done this terrible thing,' but according to the *Handbook for Advanced Apostrophe Use*, she should have written 'even though *I've* done this terrible thing.'"

"But so what?" Violet asked. "What do all these mistakes mean?"

Klaus smiled, and showed his sisters the two words he had written on the bottom of the note. "Curdled Cave," he read out loud.

"Curdled *veek*?" Sunny asked, which meant "Curdled *what*?"

"Curdled Cave," Klaus repeated. "If you take all the letters involved in the grammatical mistakes, that's what it spells. Look: C for ice instead of Ike. U for unbearable instead of inbearable. The extra R in your children instead of you children, and the extra D in dowager. L-E-D for led instead of leaded. C for act instead of akt. A for man instead of men. And V-E for I've instead of I'd. That spells CURDLED CAVE. Don't you see? Aunt Josephine *knew* she was making grammatical errors, and she knew we'd spot them. She was leaving us a message, and the message is Curdled—"

A great gust of wind interrupted Klaus as it came through the shattered window and shook the library as if it were maracas, a word which describes rattling percussion instruments used in Latin American music. Everything rattled wildly around the library as the wind flew through it. Chairs and footstools flipped over and fell to the floor with their legs in the air. The bookshelves rattled so hard that some of the heaviest books in Aunt Josephine's collection spun off into puddles of rainwater on the floor. And the Baudelaire orphans were jerked violently to the ground as a streak of lightning flashed across the darkening sky.

"Let's get out of here!" Violet shouted over the noise of the thunder, and grabbed her siblings by the hand. The wind was blowing so hard that the Baudelaires felt as if they were climbing an enormous hill instead of walking to the door of the library. The orphans were quite out of breath by the time they shut the library door behind them and stood shivering in the hallway.

"Poor Aunt Josephine," Violet said. "Her library is wrecked."

"But I need to go back in there," Klaus said, holding up the note. "We just found out what Aunt Josephine means by Curdled Cave, and we need a library to find out more."

"Not that library," Violet pointed out. "All that library had were books on grammar. We need her books on Lake Lachrymose."

"Why?" Klaus asked.

"Because I'll bet you anything that's where

Curdled Cave is," Violet said, "in Lake Lachrymose. Remember she said she knew every island in its waters and every cave on its shore? I bet Curdled Cave is one of those caves."

"But why would her secret message be about some cave?" Klaus asked.

"You've been so busy figuring out the message," Violet said, "that you don't understand what it means. Aunt Josephine isn't dead. She just wants people to *think* she's dead. But she wanted to tell *us* that she was hiding. We have to find her books on Lake Lachrymose and find out where Curdled Cave is."

"But first we have to know where the books are," Klaus said. "She told us she hid them away, remember?"

Sunny shrieked something in agreement, but her siblings couldn't hear her over a burst of thunder.

"Let's see," Violet said. "Where would you hide something if you didn't want to look at it?"

The Baudelaire orphans were quiet as they thought of places they had hidden things they did not want to look at, back when they had lived with their parents in the Baudelaire home. Violet thought of an automatic harmonica she had invented that had made such horrible noises that she had hidden it so she didn't have to think of her failure. Klaus thought of a book on the Franco-Prussian War that was so difficult that he had hidden it so as not to be reminded that he wasn't old enough to read it. And Sunny thought of a piece of stone that was too hard for even her sharpest tooth, and how she had hidden it so her jaw would no longer ache from her many attempts at conquering it. And all three Baudelaire orphans thought of the hiding place they had chosen.

"Underneath the bed," Violet said.

"Underneath the bed," Klaus agreed.

"Seeka yit," Sunny agreed, and without another word the three children ran down the hallway to Aunt Josephine's room. Normally it

is not polite to go into somebody's room without knocking, but you can make an exception
if the person is dead, or pretending to be dead,
and the Baudelaires went right inside. Aunt
Josephine's room was similar to the orphans',
with a navy-blue bedspread on the bed and
a pile of tin cans in the corner. There was a
small window looking out onto the rain-soaked
hill, and a pile of new grammar books by the
side of the bed that Aunt Josephine had not
started reading, and, I'm sad to say, would never
read. But the only part of the room that interested the children was underneath the bed,
and the three of them knelt down to look
there.

Aunt Josephine, apparently, had plenty of
things she did not want to look at anymore.
Underneath the bed there were pots and
pans, which she didn't want to look at because
they reminded her of the stove. There were
ugly socks somebody had given her as a gift
that were too ugly for human eyes. And the

Baudelaires were sad to see a framed photograph of a kind-looking man with a handful of crackers in one hand and his lips pursed as if he were whistling. It was Ike, and the Baudelaires knew that she had placed his photograph there because she was too sad to look at it. But behind one of the biggest pots was a stack of books, and the orphans immediately reached for it.

"*The Tides of Lake Lachrymose*," Violet said, reading the title of the top book. "That won't help."

"*The Bottom of Lake Lachrymose*," Klaus said, reading the next one. "That's not useful."

"*Lachrymose Trout*," Violet read.

"*The History of the Damocles Dock Region*," Klaus read.

"*Ivan Lachrymose—Lake Explorer*," Violet read.

"*How Water Is Made*," Klaus read.

"*A Lachrymose Atlas*," Violet said.

"Atlas? That's perfect!" Klaus cried. "An atlas is a book of maps!"

There was a flash of lightning outside the window, and it began to rain harder, making a sound on the roof like somebody was dropping marbles on it. Without another word the Baudelaires opened the atlas and began flipping pages. They saw map after map of the lake, but they couldn't find Curdled Cave.

"This book is four hundred seventy-eight pages long," Klaus exclaimed, looking at the last page of the atlas. "It'll take forever to find Curdled Cave."

"We don't have forever," Violet said. "Captain Sham is probably on his way here now. Use the index in the back. Look under 'Curdled.'"

Klaus flipped to the index, which I'm sure you know is an alphabetical list of each thing a book contains and what page it's on. Klaus ran his finger down the list of the C words, muttering out loud to himself. "Carp Cove, Chartreuse Island, Cloudy Cliffs, Condiment Bay, Curdled Cave—here it is! Curdled Cave, page one hundred four." Quickly Klaus flipped to the correct page and looked at the detailed map. "Curdled Cave, Curdled Cave, where is it?"

"There it is!" Violet pointed a finger at the tiny spot on the map marked *Curdled Cave.* "Directly across from Damocles Dock and just west of the Lavender Lighthouse. Let's go."

"Go?" Klaus said. "How will we get across the lake?"

"The Fickle Ferry will take us," Violet said, pointing at a dotted line on the map. "Look, the ferry goes right to the Lavender Lighthouse, and we can walk from there."

"We're going to walk to Damocles Dock, in all this rain?" Klaus asked.

"We don't have any choice," Violet answered. "We have to prove that Aunt Josephine is still alive, or else Captain Sham gets us."

"I just hope she is still—" Klaus started to say, but he stopped himself and pointed out the window. "Look!"

Violet and Sunny looked. The window in

Aunt Josephine's bedroom looked out onto the hill, and the orphans could see one of the spidery metal stilts that kept Aunt Josephine's house from falling into the lake. But they could also see that this stilt had been badly damaged by the howling storm. There was a large black burn mark, undoubtedly from lightning, and the wind had bent the stilt into an uneasy curve. As the storm raged around them, the orphans watched the stilt struggle to stay attached.

"Tafca!" Sunny shrieked, which meant "We have to get out of here *right now*!"

"Sunny's right," Violet said. "Grab the atlas and let's go."

Klaus grabbed *A Lachrymose Atlas*, not wanting to think what would be happening if they were still leafing through the book and had not looked up at the window. As the youngsters stood up, the wind rose to a feverish pitch, a phrase which here means "it shook the house and sent all three orphans toppling to the floor."

Violet fell against one of the bedposts and banged her knee. Klaus fell against the cold radiator and banged his foot. And Sunny fell into the pile of tin cans and banged everything. The whole room seemed to lurch slightly to one side as the orphans staggered back to their feet.

"Come on!" Violet screamed, and grabbed Sunny. The orphans scurried out to the hallway and toward the front door. A piece of the ceiling had come off, and rainwater was steadily pouring onto the carpet, splattering the orphans as they ran underneath it. The house gave another lurch, and the children toppled to the floor again. Aunt Josephine's house was starting to slip off the hill. "Come on!" Violet screamed again, and the orphans stumbled up the tilted hallway to the door, slipping in puddles and on their own frightened feet. Klaus was the first to reach the front door, and yanked it open as the house gave another lurch, followed by a horrible, horrible crunching sound. "Come on!"

Violet screamed again, and the Baudelaires crawled out of the door and onto the hill, huddling together in the freezing rain. They were cold. They were frightened. But they had escaped.

I have seen many amazing things in my long and troubled life history. I have seen a series of corridors built entirely out of human skulls. I have seen a volcano erupt and send a wall of lava crawling toward a small village. I have seen a woman I loved picked up by an enormous eagle and flown to its high mountain nest. But I still cannot imagine what it was like to watch Aunt Josephine's house topple into Lake Lachrymose. My own research tells me that the children watched in mute amazement as the peeling white door slammed shut and began to crumple, as you might crumple a piece of paper into a ball. I have been told that the children hugged each other even more tightly as they heard the rough and earsplitting noise of their home breaking loose from the side of the hill. But I cannot tell you how it felt to watch the whole building fall down, down, down, and hit the dark and stormy waters of the lake below.

The United States Postal Service has a motto. The motto is: "Neither rain nor sleet nor driving snow shall halt the delivery of the mails." All this means is that even when the weather is nasty and your

mailperson wants to stay inside and enjoy a cup of cocoa, he or she has to bundle up and go outside and deliver your mail anyway. The United States Postal Service does not think that icy storms should interfere with its duties.

The Baudelaire orphans were distressed to learn that the Fickle Ferry had no such policy. Violet, Klaus, and Sunny had made their way down the hill with much difficulty. The storm was rising, and the children could tell that the wind and the rain wanted nothing more than to grab them and throw them into the raging waters of Lake Lachrymose. Violet and Sunny hadn't had the time to grab their coats as they escaped the house, so all three children took turns wearing Klaus's coat as they stumbled along the flooding road. Once or twice a car drove by, and the Baudelaires had to scurry into the muddy bushes and hide, in case Captain Sham was coming to retrieve them. When they finally reached Damocles Dock, their teeth were chattering and their feet were so cold they could scarcely feel their toes, and the sight of the CLOSED sign in the window of the Fickle Ferry ticket booth was just about more than they could stand.

"It's *closed*," Klaus cried, his voice rising with despair and in order to be heard over Hurricane Herman. "How will we get to Curdled Cave now?"

"We'll have to wait until it opens," Violet replied.

"But it won't open until the storm is past," Klaus pointed out, "and by then Captain Sham will find us and take us far away. We have to get to Aunt Josephine as soon as possible."

"I don't know how we can," Violet said, shivering. "The atlas says that the cave is all the way across the lake, and we can't *swim* all that way in this weather."

"Entro!" Sunny shrieked, which meant something along the lines of "And we don't have enough time to walk around the lake, either."

"There must be other boats on this lake,"

Klaus said, "besides the ferry. Motorboats, or fishing boats, or—" He trailed off, and his eyes met those of his sisters. All three orphans were thinking the same thing.

"Or *sailboats*," Violet finished for him. "Captain Sham's Sailboat Rentals. He said it was right on Damocles Dock."

The Baudelaires stood under the awning of the ticket booth and looked down at the far end of the deserted dock, where they could see a metal gate that was very tall and had glistening spikes on the top of it. Hanging over the metal gate was a sign with some words they couldn't read, and next to the sign there was a small shack, scarcely visible in the rain, with a flickering light in the window. The children looked at it with dread in their hearts. Walking into Captain Sham's Sailboat Rentals in order to find Aunt Josephine would feel like walking into a lion's den in order to escape from a lion.

"We can't go there," Klaus said.

"We have to," Violet said. "We know Captain

Sham isn't there, because he's either on his way to Aunt Josephine's house or still at the Anxious Clown."

"But whoever *is* there," Klaus said, pointing to the flickering light, "won't let us rent a sailboat."

"They won't know we're the Baudelaires," Violet replied. "We'll tell whoever it is that we're the Jones children and that we want to go for a sail."

"In the middle of a hurricane?" Klaus replied. "They won't believe that."

"They'll have to," Violet said resolutely, a word which here means "as if she believed it, even though she wasn't so sure," and she led her siblings toward the shack. Klaus clasped the atlas close to his chest, and Sunny, whose turn it was for Klaus's coat, clutched it around herself, and soon the Baudelaires were shivering underneath the sign that read: CAPTAIN SHAM'S SAILBOAT RENTALS—EVERY BOAT HAS IT'S OWN SAIL. But the tall metal gate was locked up tight, and the Baudelaires paused there, anxious about going inside the shack.

"Let's take a look," Klaus whispered, pointing to a window, but it was too high for him or Sunny to use. Standing on tiptoe, Violet peered into the window of the shack and with one glance she knew there was no way they could rent a sailboat.

The shack was very small, with only room for a small desk and a single lightbulb, which was giving off the flickering light. But at the desk, asleep in a chair, was a person so massive that it looked like an enormous blob was in the shack, snoring away with a bottle of beer in one hand and a ring of keys in the other. As the person snored, the bottle shook, the keys jangled, and the door of the shack creaked open an inch or two, but although those noises were quite spooky, they weren't what frightened Violet. What frightened Violet was that you couldn't tell if this person was a man or a woman. There aren't very many people like that in the world, and Violet knew which one this was. Perhaps you have forgotten about Count Olaf's evil comrades, but the Baudelaires had seen them in the flesh—lots of flesh, in this comrade's case—and remembered all of them in gruesome detail. These people were rude, and they were sneaky, and they did whatever Count Olaf—or in this case, Captain Sham—told them to do, and the orphans never knew when they would turn up. And now, one had turned up right there in the shack, dangerous, treacherous, and snoring.

Violet's face must have shown her disappointment, because as soon as she took a look Klaus asked, "What's wrong? I mean, besides Hurricane Herman, and Aunt Josephine faking her own death, and Captain Sham coming after us and everything."

"One of Count Olaf's comrades is in the shack," Violet said.

"Which one?" Klaus asked.

"The one who looks like neither a man nor a woman," Violet replied.

Klaus shuddered. "That's the scariest one."

"I disagree," Violet said. "I think the bald one is scariest."

"Vass!" Sunny whispered, which probably meant "Let's discuss this at another time."

"Did he or she see you?" Klaus asked.

"No," Violet said. "He or she is asleep. But he or she is holding a ring of keys. We'll need them, I bet, to unlock the gate and get a sailboat."

"You mean we're going to steal a sailboat?" Klaus asked.

"We have no choice," Violet said. Stealing, of course, is a crime, and a very impolite thing to do. But like most impolite things, it is excusable under certain circumstances. Stealing is not excusable if, for instance, you are in a museum and you decide that a certain painting would look better in your house, and you simply grab the painting and take it there. But if you were very, very hungry, and you had no way of obtaining money, it might be excusable to grab the painting, take it to your house, and eat it. "We have to get to Curdled Cave as quickly as possible," Violet continued, "and the only way we can do it is to steal a sailboat."

"I know that," Klaus said, "but how are we going to get the keys?"

"I don't know," Violet admitted. "The door of the shack is creaky, and I'm afraid if we open it any wider we'll wake him or her up."

"You could crawl through the window," Klaus said, "by standing on my shoulders. Sunny could keep watch."

"Where *is* Sunny?" Violet asked nervously.

Violet and Klaus looked down at the ground and saw Klaus's coat sitting alone in a little heap. They looked down the dock but only saw the Fickle Ferry ticket booth and the foamy waters of the lake, darkening in the gloom of the late afternoon.

"She's gone!" Klaus cried, but Violet put a

finger to her lips and stood on tiptoe to look in the window again. Sunny was crawling through the open door of the shack, flattening her little body enough so as not to open the door any wider.

"She's inside," Violet murmured.

"In the shack?" Klaus said in a horrified gasp. "Oh no. We have to stop her."

"She's crawling very slowly toward that person," Violet said, afraid even to blink.

"We promised our parents we'd take care of her," Klaus said. "We can't let her do this."

"She's reaching toward the key ring," Violet said breathlessly. "She's gently prying it loose from the person's hand."

"Don't tell me any more," Klaus said, as a bolt of lightning streaked across the sky. "No, do tell me. What is happening?"

"She has the keys," Violet said. "She's putting them in her mouth to hold them. She's crawling back toward the door. She's flattening herself and crawling through."

"She's made it," Klaus said in amazement. Sunny came crawling triumphantly toward the orphans, the keys in her mouth. "Violet, she made it," Klaus said, giving Sunny a hug as a huge *boom!* of thunder echoed across the sky.

Violet smiled down at Sunny, but stopped smiling when she looked back into the shack. The thunder had awoken Count Olaf's comrade, and Violet watched in dismay as the person looked at its empty hand where the key ring had been, and then down on the floor where Sunny had left little crawl-prints of rainwater, and then up to the window and right into Violet's eyes.

"She's awake!" Violet shrieked. "He's awake! It's awake! Hurry, Klaus, open the gate and I'll try to distract it."

Without another word, Klaus took the key ring from Sunny's mouth and hurried to the tall metal gate. There were three keys on the ring—a skinny one, a thick one, and one with teeth as jagged as the glistening spikes hanging over the children. He put the atlas down on the ground and began to try the skinny key in the lock, just as Count Olaf's comrade came lumbering out of the shack.

Her heart in her throat, Violet stood in front of the creature and gave it a fake smile. "Good afternoon," she said, not knowing whether to add "sir" or "madam." "I seem to have gotten lost on this dock. Could you tell me the way to the Fickle Ferry?"

Count Olaf's comrade did not answer, but kept shuffling toward the orphans. The skinny key fit into the lock but didn't budge, and Klaus tried the thick one.

"I'm sorry," Violet said, "I didn't hear you. Could you tell me—"

Without a word the mountainous person grabbed Violet by the hair, and with one swing of its arm lifted her up over its smelly shoulder the way you might carry a backpack. Klaus couldn't get the thick key to fit in the lock and tried the jagged one, just as the person scooped up Sunny with its other hand and held her up, the way you might hold an ice cream cone.

"*Klaus!*" Violet screamed. "*Klaus!*"

The jagged key wouldn't fit in the lock, either. Klaus, in frustration, shook and shook the metal gate. Violet was kicking the creature from behind, and Sunny was biting its wrist, but the person was so Brobdingnagian—a word which here means "unbelievably husky"—that the children were causing it minimal pain, a phrase which here means "no pain at all." Count Olaf's comrade lumbered toward Klaus, holding the other two orphans in its grasp. In desperation, Klaus tried the skinny key again in the lock, and to his surprise and relief it turned and the tall metal gate swung open. Just a few feet away were six sailboats tied to the end of the dock with thick rope—sailboats that could take them to Aunt Josephine. But Klaus was too late. He felt something grab the back of his shirt, and he was lifted up in the air. Something slimy began running down his back, and Klaus realized with horror that the person was holding him in his or her mouth.

"Put me down!" Klaus screamed. "Put me down!"

"Put me down!" Violet yelled. "Put me down!"

"Poda rish!" Sunny shrieked. "Poda rish!"

But the lumbering creature had no concern for the wishes of the Baudelaire orphans. With great sloppy steps it turned itself around and began to carry the youngsters back toward the shack. The children heard the gloppy sound of its chubby feet sloshing through the rain, *gumsh, gumsh, gumsh, gumsh*. But then, instead of a *gumsh*, there was a *skittle-wat* as the person stepped on Aunt Josephine's atlas, which slipped from under its feet. Count Olaf's comrade waved its arms to keep its balance, dropping Violet and Sunny, and then fell to the ground, opening its mouth in surprise and dropping Klaus. The orphans, being in reasonably good physical shape, got to their feet much more quickly than this despicable creature, and ran through the open gate to the nearest sail-boat. The creature struggled to right itself and chase them, but Sunny had already bitten the rope that tied the boat to the dock. By the time the creature reached the spiky metal gate, the orphans were already on the stormy waters of Lake Lachrymose. In the dim light of the late afternoon, Klaus wiped the grime of the creature's foot off the cover of the atlas, and began to read it. Aunt Josephine's book of maps had saved them once, in showing them the location of Curdled Cave, and now it had saved them again.

CHAPTER

Ten

The good people who are publishing this book
have a concern that they have expressed to
me. The concern is that readers like yourself
will read my history of the Baudelaire
orphans and attempt to imitate some of the
things they do. So at this point in the story, in
order to mollify the publishers—the word
"mollify" here means "get them to stop
tearing their hair out in worry"—

please allow me to give you a piece of advice, even though I don't know anything about you. The piece of advice is as follows: If you ever need to get to Curdled Cave in a hurry, do not, under any circumstances, steal a boat and attempt to sail across Lake Lachrymose during a hurricane, because it is very dangerous and the chances of your survival are practically zero. You should especially not do this if, like the Baudelaire orphans, you have only a vague idea of how to work a sailboat.

Count Olaf's comrade, standing at the dock and waving a chubby fist in the air, grew smaller and smaller as the wind carried the sailboat away from Damocles Dock. As Hurricane Herman raged over them, Violet, Klaus, and Sunny examined the sailboat they had just stolen. It was fairly small, with wooden seats and bright orange life jackets for five people. On top of the mast, which is a word meaning "the tall wooden post found in the middle of boats," was a grimy white sail controlled by a series of ropes, and on the floor was a pair of wooden oars in case there was no wind. In the back, there was a sort of wooden lever with a handle for moving it this way and that, and under one of the seats was a shiny metal bucket for bailing out any water in case of a leak. There was also a long pole with a fishing net at the end of it, a small fishing rod with a sharp hook and a rusty spying glass, which is a sort of telescope used for navigating. The three siblings struggled into their life vests as the stormy waves of Lake Lachrymose took them farther and farther away from the shore.

"I read a book about working a sailboat," Klaus shouted over the noise of the hurricane. "We have to use the sail to catch the wind. Then it will push us where we want to go."

"And this lever is called a tiller," Violet shouted. "I remember it from studying some naval blueprints. The tiller controls the rudder, which is below the water, steering the ship. Sunny, sit in back and work the tiller. Klaus, hold the atlas so we can tell where we're going, and I'll try to work the sail. I think if I pull on *this* rope, I can control the sail."

Klaus turned the damp pages of the atlas to page 104. "*That* way," he called, pointing to the right. "The sun is setting over there, so that must be west."

Sunny scurried to the back of the sailboat and put her tiny hands on the tiller just as a wave hit the boat and sprayed her with foam. "Karg tem!" she called, which meant something along the lines of "I'm going to move the tiller *this* way, in order to steer the boat according to Klaus's recommendation."

The rain whipped around them, and the wind howled, and a small wave splashed over the side, but to the orphans' amazement, the sailboat moved in the exact direction they wanted it to go. If you had come across the three Baudelaires at this moment, you would have thought their lives were filled with joy and happiness, because even though they were exhausted, damp, and in very great danger, they began to laugh in their triumph. They were so relieved that something had finally gone right that they laughed as if they were at the circus instead of in the middle of a lake, in the middle of a hurricane, in the middle of trouble.

As the storm wore itself out splashing waves over the sailboat and flashing lightning over their heads, the Baudelaires sailed the tiny boat across the vast and dark lake. Violet pulled ropes this way and that to catch the wind, which kept changing direction as wind tends to do. Klaus kept a close eye on the atlas and made sure they weren't heading off course to the Wicked Whirlpool or the Rancorous Rocks. And Sunny kept the boat level by turning the tiller whenever Violet signaled. And just when the evening turned to night, and it was too dark to read the atlas, the Baudelaires saw a blinking light of pale purple. The orphans had always thought lavender was a rather sickly color, but for the first time in their lives they were glad to see it. It meant that the sailboat was approaching the

Lavender Lighthouse, and soon they'd be at Curdled Cave. The storm finally broke—the word "broke" here means "ended," rather than "shattered" or "lost all its money"—and the clouds parted to reveal an almost-full moon. The children shivered in their soaking clothes and stared out at the calming waves of the lake, watching the swirls of its inky depths.

"Lake Lachrymose is actually very pretty," Klaus said thoughtfully. "I never noticed it before."

"Cind," Sunny agreed, adjusting the tiller slightly.

"I guess we never noticed it because of Aunt Josephine," Violet said. "We got used to looking at the lake through her eyes." She picked up the spying glass and squinted into it, and she was just able to see the shore. "I think I can see the lighthouse over there. There's a dark hole in the cliff right next to it. It must be the mouth of Curdled Cave."

Sure enough, as the sailboat drew closer

and closer, the children could just make out the Lavender Lighthouse and the mouth of the nearby cave, but when they looked into its depths, they could see no sign of Aunt Josephine, or of anything else for that matter. Rocks began to scrape the bottom of the boat, which meant they were in very shallow water, and Violet jumped out to drag the sailboat onto the craggy shore. Klaus and Sunny stepped out of the boat and took off their life jackets. Then they stood at the mouth of Curdled Cave and paused nervously. In front of the cave there was a sign saying it was for sale, and the orphans could not imagine who would want to buy such a phantasmagorical—the word "phantasmagorical" here means "all the creepy, scary words you can think of put together"—place. The mouth of the cave had jagged rocks all over it like teeth in the mouth of a shark. Just beyond the entrance the youngsters could see strange white rock formations, all melted and twisted together so they looked like moldy milk. The floor of the cave was as pale and dusty as if it were made of chalk. But it was not these sights that made the children pause. It was the sound coming out of the cave. It was a high-pitched, wavering wail, a hopeless and lost sound, as strange and as eerie as Curdled Cave itself.

"What is that sound?" Violet asked nervously.

"Just the wind, probably," Klaus replied. "I read somewhere that when wind passes through small spaces, like caves, it can make weird noises. It's nothing to be afraid of."

The orphans did not move. The sound did not stop.

"I'm afraid of it, anyway," Violet said.

"Me too," Klaus said.

"Geni," Sunny said, and began to crawl into the mouth of the cave. She probably meant something along the lines of "We didn't sail a stolen sailboat across Lake Lachrymose in the middle of Hurricane Herman just to stand nervously at the mouth of a cave," and her siblings had to agree with her and follow her inside. The wailing was louder as it echoed off the walls and rock formations, and the Baudelaires could tell it wasn't the wind. It was Aunt Josephine, sitting in a corner of the cave and sobbing with her head in her hands. She was crying so hard that she hadn't even noticed the Baudelaires come into the cave.

"Aunt Josephine," Klaus said hesitantly, "we're here."

Aunt Josephine looked up, and the children could see that her face was wet from tears and chalky from the cave. "You figured it out," she said, wiping her eyes and standing up. "I knew you could figure it out," she said, and took each of the Baudelaires in her arms. She looked at Violet, and then at Klaus, and then at Sunny, and the orphans looked at her and found themselves with tears in their own eyes as they greeted their guardian. It was as if they had not quite believed that Aunt Josephine's death was fake until they had seen her alive with their own eyes.

"I knew you were clever children," Aunt Josephine said. "I knew you would read my message."

"Klaus really did it," Violet said.

"But Violet knew how to work the sailboat," Klaus said. "Without Violet we never would have arrived here."

"And Sunny stole the keys," Violet said, "and worked the tiller."

"Well, I'm glad you all made it here," Aunt Josephine said. "Let me just catch my breath and I'll help you bring in your things."

The children looked at one another. "What things?" Violet asked.

"Why, your luggage of course," Aunt Josephine replied. "And I hope you brought some food, because the supplies I brought are almost gone."

"We didn't bring any food," Klaus said.

"No food?" Aunt Josephine said. "How in the world are you going to live with me in this cave if you didn't bring any food?"

"We didn't come here to live with you," Violet said.

Aunt Josephine's hands flew to her head and she rearranged her bun nervously. "Then why are you here?" she asked.

"Stim!" Sunny shrieked, which meant "Because we were worried about you!"

"'Stim' is not a sentence, Sunny," Aunt Josephine said sternly. "Perhaps one of your older siblings could explain in correct English why you're here."

"Because Captain Sham almost had us in his clutches!" Violet cried. "Everyone thought you were dead, and you wrote in your will and testament that we should be placed in the care of Captain Sham."

"But he forced me to do that," Aunt Josephine whined. "That night, when he called me on the phone, he told me he was really Count Olaf. He said I had to write out a will saying you children would be left in his care. He said if I didn't write what he said, he would drown me in the lake. I was so frightened that I agreed immediately."

"Why didn't you call the police?" Violet asked. "Why didn't you call Mr. Poe? Why didn't you call somebody who could have helped?"

"You know why," Aunt Josephine said crossly. "I'm afraid of using the phone. Why, I was just getting used to answering it. I'm nowhere near ready to use the numbered buttons. But in any case, I didn't need to call anybody. I threw a footstool through the window and then sneaked out of the house. I left you the note so that you would know I wasn't really dead, but I hid my message so that Captain Sham wouldn't know I had escaped from him."

"Why didn't you take us with you? Why did you leave us all alone by ourselves? Why didn't you protect us from Captain Sham?" Klaus asked.

"It is not grammatically correct," Aunt Josephine said, "to say 'leave us all alone by ourselves.' You can say 'leave us all alone,' or 'leave us by ourselves,' but not both. Do you understand?"

The Baudelaires looked at one another in sadness and anger. They understood. They understood that Aunt Josephine was more concerned with grammatical mistakes than with saving the lives of the three children. They understood that she was so wrapped up in her own fears that she had not given a thought to what might have happened to them. They understood that Aunt Josephine had been a terrible guardian, in leaving the children all by themselves in great danger. They understood and they wished more than ever that their parents, who never would have run away and left them alone, had not been killed in that terrible fire which had begun all the misfortune in the Baudelaire lives.

"Well, enough grammar lessons for today," Aunt Josephine said. "I'm happy to see you, and you are welcome to share this cave with me.

I don't think Captain Sham will ever find us here."

"We're not *staying here*," Violet said impatiently. "We're sailing back to town, and we're taking you with us."

"No way, José," Aunt Josephine said, using an expression which means "No way" and has nothing to do with José, whoever he is. "I'm too frightened of Captain Sham to face him. After all he's done to you I would think that you would be frightened of him, too."

"We *are* frightened of him," Klaus said, "but if we prove that he's really Count Olaf he will go to jail. You are the proof. If you tell Mr. Poe what happened, then Count Olaf will be locked away and we will be safe."

"You can tell him, if you want to," Aunt Josephine said. "I'm staying here."

"He won't believe us unless you come with us and prove that you're alive," Violet said.

"No, no, no," Aunt Josephine said. "I'm too afraid."

Violet took a deep breath and faced her frightened guardian. "We're *all* afraid," she said firmly. "We were afraid when we met Captain Sham in the grocery store. We were afraid when we thought that you had jumped out the window. We were afraid to give ourselves allergic reactions, and we were afraid to steal a sailboat and we were afraid to make our way across this lake in the middle of a hurricane. But that didn't stop us."

Aunt Josephine's eyes filled up with tears. "I can't help it that you're braver than I," she said. "I'm not sailing across that lake. I'm not making any phone calls. I'm going to stay right here for the rest of my life, and nothing you can say will change my mind."

Klaus stepped forward and played his trump card, a phrase which means "said something very convincing, which he had saved for the end of the argument." "Curdled Cave," he said, "is for sale."

"So what?" Aunt Josephine said.

"That means," Klaus said, "that before long certain people will come to look at it. And some of those people"—he paused here dramatically—"will be realtors."

Aunt Josephine's mouth hung open, and the orphans watched her pale throat swallow in fear. "Okay," she said finally, looking around the cave anxiously as if a realtor were already hiding in the shadows. "I'll go."

"*Oh* no," Aunt Josephine said.

The children paid no attention. The worst of Hurricane Herman was over, and as the Baudelaires sailed across the dark lake there seemed to be very little danger. Violet moved the sail around with ease now that the wind was calm. Klaus looked back at the lavender light of the lighthouse and confidently guided the way back to Damocles Dock. And Sunny moved the tiller as if she had been a tillermover all her life. Only Aunt Josephine was scared. She was wearing two life jackets instead of one, and every few seconds she cried "Oh no," even though nothing frightening was happening.

"Oh no," Aunt Josephine said, "and I mean it this time."

"What's wrong, Aunt Josephine?" Violet said tiredly. The sailboat had reached the approximate middle of the lake. The water was still fairly calm, and the lighthouse still glowed, a pinpoint of pale purple light. There seemed to be no cause for alarm.

"We're about to enter the territory of the Lachrymose Leeches," Aunt Josephine said.

"I'm sure we'll pass through safely," Klaus said, peering through the spying glass to see if Damocles Dock was visible yet. "You told us that the leeches were harmless and only preyed on small fish."

"Unless you've eaten recently," Aunt Josephine said.

"But it's been hours since we've eaten," Violet said soothingly. "The last thing we ate were peppermints at the Anxious Clown. That was in the afternoon, and now it's the middle of the night."

Aunt Josephine looked down, and moved away from the side of the boat. "But I ate a banana," she whispered, "just before you arrived."

"Oh no," Violet said. Sunny stopped moving the tiller and looked worriedly into the water.

"I'm sure there's nothing to worry about," Klaus said. "Leeches are very small animals. If we were in the water, we might have reason to fear, but I don't think they'd attack a sailboat. Plus, Hurricane Herman may have frightened them away from their territory. I bet the Lachrymose Leeches won't even show up."

Klaus thought he was done speaking for the moment, but in the moment that followed he added one more sentence. The sentence was "Speak of the Devil," and it is an expression that you use when you are talking about something only to have it occur. For instance, if you were at a picnic and said, "I hope it doesn't snow," and at that very minute a blizzard began, you could say, "Speak of the Devil" before gathering up your blanket and potato salad and driving away to a good restaurant. But in the case of the Baudelaire orphans, I'm sure you can guess what happened to prompt Klaus to use this expression.

"Speak of the Devil," Klaus said, looking into the waters of the lake. Out of the swirling blackness came skinny, rising shapes, barely visible in the moonlight. The shapes were scarcely longer than a finger, and at first it looked as if someone were swimming in the lake and drumming their fingers on the surface of the water. But most people have only ten fingers, and in the few minutes that followed there were hundreds of these tiny shapes, wriggling hungrily from all sides toward the sailboat. The Lachrymose Leeches made a quiet, whispering sound on the water as they swam, as if the Baudelaire orphans were surrounded by people murmuring terrible secrets. The children watched in silence as the swarm approached the boat, each leech knocking lightly against the wood. Their tiny leech-mouths puckered in disappointment as they tried to taste the sailboat. Leeches are blind, but they aren't stupid, and the Lachrymose Leeches knew that they were not eating a banana.

"You see?" Klaus said nervously, as the tapping of leech-mouths continued. "We're perfectly safe."

"Yes," Violet said. She wasn't sure they were perfectly safe, not at all, but it seemed best to tell Aunt Josephine they were perfectly safe. "We're perfectly safe," she said.

The tapping sound continued, getting a little rougher and louder. Frustration is an interesting emotional state, because it tends to bring out the worst in whoever is frustrated. Frustrated babies tend to throw food and make a mess. Frustrated citizens tend to execute kings and queens and make a democracy. And frustrated moths tend to bang up against lightbulbs and make light fixtures all dusty. But unlike babies, citizens, and moths, leeches are quite unpleasant to begin with. Now that the Lachrymose Leeches were getting frustrated, everyone on board the sailboat was quite anxious to see what would happen when frustration brought out the worst in leeches. For a while, the small creatures tried and tried to eat the wood, but their tiny teeth didn't really do anything but make an unpleasant knocking sound. But then, all at once, the leeches knocked off, and the Baudelaires watched them wriggle away from the sailboat.

"They're leaving," Klaus said hopefully, but they weren't leaving. When the leeches had reached a considerable distance, they suddenly swiveled their tiny bodies around and came rushing back to the boat. With a loud *thwack!* the leeches all hit the boat more or less at once, and the sailboat rocked precariously, a word which here means "in a way which almost threw Aunt

Josephine and the Baudelaire youngsters to their doom." The four passengers were rocked to and fro and almost fell into the waters of the lake, where the leeches were wriggling away again to prepare for another attack.

"Yadec!" Sunny shrieked and pointed at the side of the boat. Yadec, of course, is not grammatically correct English, but even Aunt Josephine understood that the youngest Baudelaire meant "Look at the crack in the boat that the leeches have made!" The crack was a tiny one, about as long as a pencil and about as wide as a human hair, and it was curved downward so it looked as if the sailboat were frowning at them. If the leeches kept hitting the side of the boat, the frown would only get wider.

"We have to sail much faster," Klaus said, "or this boat will be in pieces in no time."

"But sailing relies on the wind," Violet pointed out. "We can't make the wind go faster."

"I'm frightened!" Aunt Josephine cried. "Please don't throw me overboard!"

"Nobody's going to throw you overboard," Violet said impatiently, although I'm sorry to tell you that Violet was wrong about that. "Take an oar, Aunt Josephine. Klaus, take the other one. If we use the sail, the tiller, *and* the oars we should move more quickly."

Thwack! The Lachrymose Leeches hit the side of the boat, widening the crack in the side and rocking the boat again. One of the leeches was thrown over the side in the impact, and twisted this way and that on the floor of the boat, gnashing its tiny teeth as it looked for food. Grimacing, Klaus walked cautiously over to it and tried to kick the leech overboard, but it clung onto his shoe and began gnawing through the leather. With a cry of disgust, Klaus shook his leg, and the leech fell to the floor of the sailboat again, stretching its tiny neck and opening and shutting its mouth. Violet grabbed the long pole with the net at the end of it, scooped up the leech, and tossed it overboard.

Thwack! The crack widened enough that a bit

of water began to dribble through, making a small puddle on the sailboat's floor. "Sunny," Violet said, "keep an eye on that puddle. When it gets bigger, use the bucket to throw it back in the lake."

"Mofee!" Sunny shrieked, which meant "I certainly will." There was the whispering sound as the leeches swam away to ram the boat again. Klaus and Aunt Josephine began rowing as hard as they could, while Violet adjusted the sail and kept the net in her hand for any more leeches who got on board.

Thwack! Thwack! There were two loud noises now, one on the side of the boat and one on the bottom, which cracked immediately. The leeches had divided up into two teams, which is good news for playing kickball but bad news if you are being attacked. Aunt Josephine gave a shriek of terror. Water was now leaking into the sailboat in two spots, and Sunny abandoned the tiller to bail the water back out. Klaus stopped rowing, and held the oar up without a word. It had several small bite marks in it—the work of the Lachrymose Leeches.

"Rowing isn't going to work," he reported to Violet solemnly. "If we row any more these oars will be completely eaten."

Violet watched Sunny crawl around with the bucket full of water. "Rowing won't help us, anyway," she said. "This boat is sinking. We need help."

Klaus looked around at the dark and still waters, empty except for the sailboat and swarms of leeches. "Where can we get help in the middle of a lake?" he asked.

"We're going to have to signal for help," Violet said, and reached into her pocket and took out a ribbon. Handing Klaus the fishing net, she used the ribbon to tie her hair up, keeping it out of her eyes. Klaus and Sunny watched her, knowing that she only tied her hair up this way when she was thinking of an invention, and right now they needed an invention quite desperately.

"That's right," Aunt Josephine said to Violet, "close your eyes. That's what I do when I'm afraid, and it always makes me feel better to block out the fear."

"She's not blocking out anything," Klaus said crossly. "She's concentrating."

Klaus was right. Violet concentrated as hard as she could, racking her brain for a good way to signal for help. She thought of fire alarms. With flashing lights and loud sirens, fire alarms were an excellent way to signal for assistance. Although the Baudelaire orphans, of course, sadly knew that sometimes the fire engines arrived too late to save people's lives, a fire alarm was still a good invention, and Violet tried to think of a way she could imitate it using the materials around her. She needed to make a loud sound, to get somebody's attention. And she needed to make a bright light, so that person would know where they were.

Thwack! Thwack! The two teams of leeches hit the boat again, and there was a splash as more water came pouring into the sailboat. Sunny started to fill the bucket with water, but Violet reached forward and took it from Sunny's hands. "Bero?" Sunny shrieked, which meant "Are you crazy?" but Violet had no time to answer "No, as a matter of fact I'm not." So she merely said "No," and, holding the bucket in one hand, began to climb up the mast. It is difficult enough to climb up the mast of a boat, but it is triple the difficulty if the boat is being rocked by a bunch of hungry leeches, so allow me to advise you that this is another thing that you should under no circumstances try to do. But Violet Baudelaire was a wunderkind, a German word which here means "someone who is able to quickly climb masts on boats being attacked by leeches," and soon she was on the top of the swaying mast of the boat. She took the bucket and hung it by its handle on the tip of the mast so it swung this way and that, the way a bell might do in a bell tower.

"I don't mean to interrupt you," Klaus called, scooping up a furious leech in the net and tossing it as far as he could, "but this boat is really sinking. Please hurry."

Violet hurried. Hurriedly, she grabbed ahold of a corner of the sail and, taking a deep breath to prepare herself, jumped back down to the floor of the boat. Just as she had hoped, the sail ripped as she hurtled to the ground, slowing her down and leaving her with a large piece of torn cloth. By now the sailboat had quite a lot of water in it, and Violet splashed over to Aunt Josephine, avoiding the many leeches that Klaus was tossing out of the boat as quickly as he could.

"I need your oar," Violet said, wadding the piece of sail up into a ball, "and your hairnet."

"You can have the oar," Aunt Josephine said, handing it over. "But I need my hairnet. It keeps my bun in place."

"Give her the hairnet!" Klaus cried, hopping up on one of the seats as a leech tried to bite his knee.

"But I'm scared of having hair in my face," Aunt Josephine whined, just as another pair of *thwack!*s hit the boat.

"I don't have time to argue with you!" Violet cried. "I'm trying to save each of our lives! Give me your hairnet right now!"

"The expression," Aunt Josephine said, "is saving *all of our lives*, not *each of our lives*," but Violet had heard enough. Splashing forward and avoiding a pair of wriggling leeches, the eldest Baudelaire reached forward and grabbed Aunt Josephine's hairnet off of her head. She wrapped the crumpled part of the sail in the hairnet, and then grabbed the fishing pole and attached the messy ball of cloth to the fishhook. It looked like she was about to go fishing for some kind of fish that liked sailboats and hair accessories for food.

Thwack! Thwack! The sailboat tilted to one side and then to the other. The leeches had almost smashed their way through the side. Violet took the oar and began to rub it up and down the side of the boat as fast and as hard as she could.

"What are you doing?" Klaus asked, catching three leeches in one swoop of his net.

"I'm trying to create friction," Violet said. "If I rub two pieces of wood enough, I'll create friction. Friction creates sparks. When I get a spark, I'll set the cloth and hairnet on fire and use it as a signal."

"You want to set a fire?" Klaus cried. "But a fire will mean more danger."

"Not if I wave the fire over my head, using the fishing pole," Violet said. "I'll do that, and hit the bucket like a bell, and that should create enough of a signal to fetch us some help." She rubbed and rubbed the oar against the side of the boat, but no sparks appeared. The sad truth was that the wood was too wet from Hurricane Herman and from Lake Lachrymose to create enough friction to start a fire. It was a good idea, but Violet realized, as she rubbed and rubbed without any result, that it was the wrong idea.

Thwack! Thwack! Violet looked around at Aunt Josephine and her terrified siblings and felt hope leak out of her heart as quickly as water was leaking into the boat. "It's not working," Violet said miserably, and felt tears fall down her cheeks. She thought of the promise she made to her parents, shortly before they were killed, that she would always take care of her younger siblings. The leeches swarmed around the sinking boat, and Violet feared that she had not lived up to her promise. "It's not working," she said again, and dropped the oar in despair. "We need a fire, but I can't invent one."

"It's okay," Klaus said, even though of course it was not. "We'll think of something."

"Tintet," Sunny said, which meant something along the lines of "Don't cry. You tried your best," but Violet cried anyway. It is very easy to say that the important thing is to try your best, but if you are in real trouble the most important thing is not trying your best, but getting to safety. The boat rocked back and forth,

and water poured through the cracks, and Violet
cried because it looked like they would never
get to safety. Her shoulders shaking with sobs,
she held the spying glass up to her eye to see if,
by any chance, there was a boat nearby, or if the
tide had happened to carry the sailboat to shore,
but all she could see was the moonlight reflect-
ing on the rippling waters of the lake. And this
was a lucky thing. Because as soon as Violet saw
the flickering reflection, she remembered the
scientific principles of the convergence and
refraction of light.

The scientific principles of the convergence
and refraction of light are very confusing, and
quite frankly I can't make head or tail of them,
even when my friend Dr. Lorenz explains them
to me. But they made perfect sense to Violet.
Instantly, she thought of a story her father had
told her, long ago, when she was just beginning
to be interested in science. When her father was
a boy, he'd had a dreadful cousin who liked to
burn ants, starting a fire by focusing the light

of the sun with her magnifying glass. Burning ants, of course, is an abhorrent hobby—the word "abhorrent" here means "what Count Olaf used to do when he was about your age"—but remembering the story made Violet see that she could use the lens of the spying glass to focus the light of the moon and make a fire. Without wasting another moment, she grabbed the spying glass and removed the lens, and then, looking up at the moon, tilted the lens at an angle she hastily computed in her head.

The moonlight passed through the lens and was concentrated into a long, thin band of light, like a glowing thread leading right to the piece of sail, held in a ball by Aunt Josephine's hair-net. In a moment the thread had become a small flame.

"It's miraculous!" Klaus cried, as the flame took hold.

"It's unbelievable!" Aunt Josephine cried.

"Fonti!" Sunny shrieked.

"It's the scientific principles of the convergence and refraction of light!" Violet cried, wiping her eyes. Stepping carefully to avoid onboard leeches and so as not to put out the fire, she moved to the front of the boat. With one hand, she took the oar and rang the bucket, making a loud sound to get somebody's attention. With the other hand, she held the fishing rod up high, making a bright light so the person would know where they were. Violet looked up at her homemade signaling device that had finally caught fire, all because of a silly story her father had told her. Her father's ant-burning cousin sounded like a dreadful person, but if she had suddenly appeared on the sailboat Violet would have given her a big grateful hug.

As it turned out, however, this signal was a mixed blessing, a phrase which means "something half good and half bad." Somebody saw the signal almost immediately, somebody who was already sailing in the lake, and who headed toward the Baudelaires in an instant. Violet, Klaus, Sunny, and even Aunt Josephine all grinned as they saw another boat sail into view. They were being rescued, and that was the good half. But their smiles began to fade as the boat drew closer and they saw who was sailing it. Aunt Josephine and the orphans saw the wooden peg leg, and the navy-blue sailor cap, and the eye patch, and they knew who was coming to their aid. It was Captain Sham, of course, and he was probably the worst half in the world.

CHAPTER Twelve

"*Welcome* aboard," Captain Sham said, with a wicked grin that showed his filthy teeth. "I'm happy to see you all. I thought you had been killed when the old lady's house fell off the hill, but luckily my associate told me you had stolen a boat and run away. And you, Josephine—I thought you'd done the sensible thing and jumped out the window."

"I tried to do the sensible

thing," Aunt Josephine said sourly. "But these children came and got me."

Captain Sham smiled. He had expertly steered his sailboat so it was alongside the one the Baudelaires had stolen, and Aunt Josephine and the children had stepped over the swarming leeches to come aboard. With a gurgly *whoosh!* their own sailboat was overwhelmed with water and quickly sank into the depths of the lake. The Lachrymose Leeches swarmed around the sinking sailboat, gnashing their tiny teeth. "Aren't you going to say thank you, orphans?" Captain Sham asked, pointing to the swirling place in the lake where their sailboat had been. "If it weren't for me, all of you would be divided up into the stomachs of those leeches."

"If it weren't for you," Violet said fiercely, "we wouldn't be in Lake Lachrymose to begin with."

"You can blame *that* on the old woman," he said, pointing to Aunt Josephine. "Faking your own death was pretty clever, but not clever enough. The Baudelaire fortune—and, unfortunately, the brats who come with it—now belong to me."

"Don't be ridiculous," Klaus said. "We don't belong to you and we never will. Once we tell Mr. Poe what happened he will send you to jail."

"Is that so?" Captain Sham said, turning the sailboat around and sailing toward Damocles Dock. His one visible eye was shining brightly as if he were telling a joke. "Mr. Poe will send me to jail, eh? Why, Mr. Poe is putting finishing touches on your adoption papers this very moment. In a few hours, you orphans will be Violet, Klaus, and Sunny Sham."

"Neihab!" Sunny shrieked, which meant "I'm Sunny Baudelaire, and I will always be Sunny Baudelaire unless I decide for myself to legally change my name!"

"When we explain that you forced Aunt Josephine to write that note," Violet said,

"Mr. Poe will rip up those adoption papers into a thousand pieces."

"Mr. Poe won't believe you," Captain Sham said, chuckling. "Why should he believe three runaway pipsqueaks who go around stealing boats?"

"Because we're telling the truth!" Klaus cried.

"Truth, schmuth," Captain Sham said. If you don't care about something, one way to demonstrate your feelings is to say the word and then repeat the word with the letters S-C-H-M replacing the real first letters. Somebody who didn't care about dentists, for instance, could say "Dentists, schmentists." But only a despicable person like Captain Sham wouldn't care about the truth. "Truth, schmuth," he said again. "I think Mr. Poe is more likely to believe the owner of a respectable sailboat rental place, who went out in the middle of a hurricane to rescue three ungrateful boat thieves."

"We only stole the boat," Violet said, "to

retrieve Aunt Josephine from her hiding place
so she could tell everyone about your terrible
plan."

"But nobody will believe the old woman,
either," Captain Sham said impatiently. "Nobody
believes a dead woman."

"Are you blind in *both* eyes?" Klaus asked.
"Aunt Josephine isn't dead!"

Captain Sham smiled again, and looked out
at the lake. Just a few yards away the water
was rippling as the Lachrymose Leeches swam
toward Captain Sham's sailboat. After search-
ing every inch of the Baudelaires' boat and fail-
ing to find any food, the leeches had realized
they had been tricked and were once again
following the scent of banana still lingering on
Aunt Josephine. "She's not dead *yet*," Captain
Sham said, in a terrible voice, and took a step
toward her.

"Oh no," she said. Her eyes were wide with
fear. "Don't throw me overboard," she pleaded.
"Please!"

"You're not going to reveal my plan to Mr. Poe," Captain Sham said, taking another step toward the terrified woman, "because you will be joining your beloved Ike at the bottom of the lake."

"No she won't," Violet said, grabbing a rope. "I will steer us to shore before you can do anything about it."

"I'll help," Klaus said, running to the back and grabbing the tiller.

"Igal!" Sunny shrieked, which meant something along the lines of "And I'll guard Aunt Josephine." She crawled in front of the Baudelaires' guardian and bared her teeth at Captain Sham.

"I promise not to say anything to Mr. Poe!" Aunt Josephine said desperately. "I'll go someplace and hide away, and never show my face! You can tell him I'm dead! You can have the fortune! You can have the children! Just don't throw me to the leeches!"

The Baudelaires looked at their guardian in

horror. "You're supposed to be caring for us," Violet told Aunt Josephine in astonishment, "not putting us up for grabs!"

Captain Sham paused, and seemed to consider Aunt Josephine's offer. "You have a point," he said. "I don't necessarily have to kill you. People just have to *think* that you're dead."

"I'll change my name!" Aunt Josephine said. "I'll dye my hair! I'll wear colored contact lenses! And I'll go very, very far away! Nobody will ever hear from me!"

"But what about us, Aunt Josephine?" Klaus asked in horror. "What about *us*?"

"Be quiet, orphan," Captain Sham snapped. The Lachrymose Leeches reached the sailboat and began tapping on the wooden side. "The adults are talking. Now, old woman, I wish I could believe you. But you hadn't been a very trustworthy person."

"*Haven't* been," Aunt Josephine corrected, wiping a tear from her eye.

"What?" Captain Sham asked.

"You made a grammatical error," Aunt Josephine said. "You said 'But you hadn't been a very trustworthy person,' but you should have said, 'you *haven't* been a very trustworthy person.'"

Captain Sham's one shiny eye blinked, and his mouth curled up in a terrible smile. "Thank you for pointing that out," he said, and took one last step toward Aunt Josephine. Sunny growled at him, and he looked down and in one swift gesture moved his peg leg and knocked Sunny to the other end of his boat. "Let me make sure I completely understand the grammatical lesson," he said to the Baudelaires' trembling guardian, as if nothing had happened. "You wouldn't say 'Josephine Anwhistle *had* been thrown overboard to the leeches,' because that would be incorrect. But if you said 'Josephine Anwhistle *has* been thrown overboard to the leeches,' that would be all right with you."

"Yes," Aunt Josephine said. "I mean *no*. I mean—"

But Aunt Josephine never got to say what she meant. Captain Sham faced her and, using both hands, pushed her over the side of the boat. With a little gasp and a big splash she fell into the waters of Lake Lachrymose.

"*Aunt Josephine!*" Violet cried. "*Aunt Josephine!*"

Klaus leaned over the side of the boat and stretched his hand out as far as he could. Thanks to her two life jackets, Aunt Josephine was floating on top of the water, waving her hands in the air as the leeches swam toward her. But Captain Sham was already pulling at the ropes of the sail, and Klaus couldn't reach her. "You *fiend*!" he shouted at Captain Sham. "You evil fiend!"

"That's no way to talk to your father," Captain Sham said calmly.

Violet tried to tug a rope out of Captain Sham's hand. "Move the sailboat back!" she shouted. "Turn the boat around!"

"Not a chance," he replied smoothly. "Wave

good-bye to the old woman, orphans. You'll never see her again."

Klaus leaned over as far as he could. "Don't worry, Aunt Josephine!" he called, but his voice revealed that he was very worried himself. The boat was already quite a ways from Aunt Josephine, and the orphans could only see the white of her hands as she waved them over the dark water.

"She has a chance," Violet said quietly to Klaus as they sailed toward the dock. "She has those life jackets, and she's a strong swimmer."

"That's true," Klaus said, his voice shaky and sad. "She's lived by the lake her whole life. Maybe she knows of an escape route."

"Legru," Sunny said quietly, which meant "All we can do is hope."

The three orphans huddled together, shivering in cold and fear, as Captain Sham sailed the boat by himself. They didn't dare do anything but hope. Their feelings for Aunt Josephine were all a tumble in their minds. The

Baudelaires had not really enjoyed most of their
time with her—not because she cooked horrible cold meals, or chose presents for them that
they didn't like, or always corrected the children's grammar, but because she was so afraid
of everything that she made it impossible to
really enjoy anything at all. And the worst of
it was, Aunt Josephine's fear had made her a
bad guardian. A guardian is supposed to stay
with children and keep them safe, but Aunt
Josephine had run away at the first sign of
danger. A guardian is supposed to help children
in times of trouble, but Aunt Josephine practically had to be dragged out of the Curdled Cave
when they needed her. And a guardian is supposed to protect children from danger, but Aunt
Josephine had offered the orphans to Captain
Sham in exchange for her own safety.

But despite all of Aunt Josephine's faults, the
orphans still cared about her. She had taught
them many things, even if most of them were
boring. She had provided a home, even if it was

cold and unable to withstand hurricanes. And the children knew that Aunt Josephine, like the Baudelaires themselves, had experienced some terrible things in her life. So as their guardian faded from view and the lights of Damocles Dock approached closer and closer, Violet, Klaus, and Sunny did not think "Josephine, schmosephine." They thought "We hope Aunt Josephine is safe."

Captain Sham sailed the boat right up to the shore and tied it expertly to the dock. "Come along, little idiots," he said, and led the Baudelaires to the tall metal gate with the glistening spikes on top, where Mr. Poe was waiting with his handkerchief in his hand and a look of relief on his face. Next to Mr. Poe was the Brobdingnagian creature, who gazed at them with a triumphant expression on his or her face.

"You're safe!" Mr. Poe said. "Thank goodness! We were so worried about you! When Captain Sham and I reached the Anwhistle home and saw that it had fallen into the sea, we thought you were done for!"

"It is lucky my associate told me that they had stolen a sailboat," Captain Sham told Mr. Poe. "The boat was nearly destroyed by Hurricane Herman, and by a swarm of leeches. I rescued them just in time."

"He did not!" Violet shouted. "He threw Aunt Josephine into the lake! We have to go and rescue her!"

"The children are upset and confused," Captain Sham said, his eye shining. "As their father, I think they need a good night's sleep."

"He's not our father!" Klaus shouted. "He's Count Olaf, and he's a murderer! Please, Mr. Poe, alert the police! We have to save Aunt Josephine!"

"Oh, dear," Mr. Poe said, coughing into his handkerchief. "You certainly *are* confused, Klaus. Aunt Josephine is dead, remember? She threw herself out the window."

"No, no," Violet said. "Her suicide note had a secret message in it. Klaus decoded the note and it said 'Curdled Cave.' Actually, it said 'apostrophe Curdled Cave,' but the apostrophe was just to get our attention."

"You're not making any sense," Mr. Poe said. "What cave? What apostrophe?"

"Klaus," Violet said, "show Mr. Poe the note."

"You can show it to him in the morning," Captain Sham said, in a falsely soothing tone. "You need a good night's sleep. My associate will take you to my apartment while I stay here and finish the adoption paperwork with Mr. Poe."

"But—" Klaus said.

"But nothing," Captain Sham said. "You're very distraught, which means 'upset.'"

"I *know* what it means," Klaus said.

"*Please* listen to us," Violet begged Mr. Poe. "It's a matter of life or death. *Please* just take a look at the note."

"You can show it to him," Captain Sham said, his voice rising in anger, "*in the morning.* Now please follow my associate to my minivan and go straight to bed."

"Hold on a minute, Captain Sham," Mr. Poe said. "If it upsets the children so much, I'll take a look at the note. It will only take a moment."

"Thank you," Klaus said in relief, and reached into his pocket for the note. But as soon as he reached inside his face fell in disappointment, and I'm sure you can guess why. If you place a piece of paper in your pocket, and then soak yourself in a hurricane, the piece of paper, no matter how important it is, will turn into a soggy mess. Klaus pulled a damp lump out of his pocket, and the orphans looked at the remains of Aunt Josephine's note. You could scarcely tell that it had been a piece of paper, let alone read the note or the secret it contained.

"This *was* the note," Klaus said, holding it out to Mr. Poe. "You'll just have to take our word for it that Aunt Josephine was still alive."

"And she might *still* be alive!" Violet cried. "*Please*, Mr. Poe, send someone to rescue her!"

"Oh my, children," Mr. Poe said. "You're so sad and worried. But you don't have to worry anymore. I have always promised to provide for you, and I think Captain Sham will do an excellent job of raising you. He has a steady business and doesn't seem likely to throw himself out of a window. And it's obvious he cares for you very much—why, he went out alone, in the middle of a hurricane, to search for you."

"The only thing he cares about," Klaus said bitterly, "is our fortune."

"Why, that's not true," Captain Sham said. "I don't want a penny of your fortune. Except, of course, to pay for the sailboat you stole and wrecked."

Mr. Poe frowned, and coughed into his handkerchief. "Well, that's a surprising request," he said, "but I suppose that can be arranged. Now, children, please go to your new home while I make the final arrangements with Captain Sham. Perhaps we'll have time for breakfast tomorrow before I head back to the city."

"*Please,*" Violet cried. "*Please,* won't you listen to us?"

"*Please,*" Klaus cried. "*Please,* won't you believe us?"

Sunny did not say anything. Sunny had not said anything for a long time, and if her siblings hadn't been so busy trying to reason with Mr. Poe, they would have noticed that she wasn't even looking up to watch everyone talking. During this whole conversation, Sunny was looking straight ahead, and if you are a baby this means looking at people's legs. The leg she was looking at was Captain Sham's. She wasn't looking at his right leg, which was perfectly normal, but at his peg leg. She was looking at the stump of dark polished wood, attached to his left knee with a curved metal hinge, and concentrating very hard.

It may surprise you to learn that at this moment, Sunny resembled the famous Greek conqueror Alexander the Great. Alexander the Great lived more than two thousand years ago, and his last name was not actually "The Great." "The Great" was something that he forced people to call him, by bringing a bunch of soldiers into their land and proclaiming himself king. Besides invading other people's countries and forcing them to do whatever he said, Alexander the Great was famous for something called the Gordian Knot. The Gordian Knot was a fancy knot tied in a piece of rope by a king named Gordius. Gordius said that if Alexander could untie it, he could rule the whole kingdom. But Alexander, who was too busy conquering places to learn how to untie knots, simply drew his sword and cut the Gordian Knot in two. This was cheating, of course, but Alexander had too many soldiers for Gordius to argue, and soon everybody in Gordium had to bow down to You-Know-Who the Great. Ever since then, a difficult problem can be called a Gordian Knot, and if you solve the problem in a simple way— even if the way is rude—you are cutting the Gordian Knot.

The problem the Baudelaire orphans were experiencing could certainly be called a Gordian Knot, because it looked impossible to solve. The problem, of course, was that Captain Sham's despicable plan was about to succeed, and the way to solve it was to convince Mr. Poe of what was really going on. But with Aunt Josephine thrown in the lake, and her note a ruined lump of wet paper, Violet and Klaus were unable to convince Mr. Poe of anything. Sunny, however, stared at Captain Sham's peg leg and thought of a simple, if rude, way of solving the problem.

As all the taller people argued and paid no attention to Sunny, the littlest Baudelaire crawled as close as she could to the peg leg, opened her mouth and bit down as hard as she could. Luckily for the Baudelaires, Sunny's teeth were as sharp as the sword of Alexander the Great, and Captain Sham's peg leg split right in half with a *crack!* that made everybody look down.

As I'm sure you've guessed, the peg leg was fake, and it split open to reveal Captain Sham's real leg, pale and sweaty from knee to toes. But it was neither the knee nor the toes that interested everyone. It was the ankle. For there on the pale and sweaty skin of Captain Sham was the solution to their problem. By biting the peg leg, Sunny had cut the Gordian Knot, for as the wooden pieces of fake peg leg fell to the floor of Damocles Dock, everyone could see a tattoo of an eye.

Mr. Poe looked astonished. Violet looked relieved. Klaus looked assuaged, which is a fancy word for "relieved" that he had learned by reading a magazine article. Sunny looked triumphant. The person who looked like neither a man nor a woman looked disappointed. And Count Olaf—it is such a relief to call him by his true name—at first looked afraid, but in a blink of his one shiny eye, he twisted his face to make it look as astonished as Mr. Poe's.

"My leg!" Count Olaf cried, in a voice of false joy. "My leg has grown back! It's amazing! It's wonderful! It's a medical miracle!"

"Oh come now," Mr. Poe said, folding his arms. "That won't work. Even a child can see that your peg leg was false."

"A child *did* see it," Violet whispered to Klaus. "*Three* children, in fact."

"Well, maybe the peg leg was false," Count Olaf admitted, and took a step backward. "But I've never seen this tattoo in my life."

"Oh come now," Mr. Poe said again. "That won't work, either. You tried to hide the tattoo with the peg leg, but now we can see that you are really Count Olaf."

"Well, maybe the tattoo is mine," Count Olaf admitted, and took another step backward. "But I'm not this Count Olaf person. I'm Captain Sham. See, I have a business card here that says so."

"Oh come now," Mr. Poe said yet again. "That won't work. Anyone can go to a print shop and have cards made that say anything they like."

"Well, maybe I'm not Captain Sham," Count Olaf admitted, "but the children still belong to me. Josephine said that they did."

"Oh come now," Mr. Poe said for the fourth and final time. "That won't work. Aunt Josephine left the children to Captain Sham, not to Count Olaf. And you are Count Olaf, not Captain Sham. So it is once again up to me to decide who will care for the Baudelaires. I will send these three youngsters somewhere else, and I will send you to jail. You have performed your evil deeds for the last time, Olaf. You tried to steal the Baudelaire fortune by marrying Violet. You tried to steal the Baudelaire fortune by murdering Uncle Monty."

"And this," Count Olaf growled, "was my greatest plan yet." He reached up and tore off his eyepatch—which was fake, of course, like his peg leg—and stared at the Baudelaires with both of his shiny eyes. "I don't like to brag—actually, why should I lie to you fools any-more?—I *love* to brag, and forcing that stupid old woman to write that note was really some-thing to brag about. What a ninny Josephine was!"

"She was not a ninny!" Klaus cried. "She was kind and sweet!"

"*Sweet?*" Count Olaf repeated, with a hor-rible smile. "Well, at this very moment the Lachrymose Leeches are probably finding her very sweet indeed. She might be the sweetest breakfast they ever ate."

Mr. Poe frowned, and coughed into his white handkerchief. "That's enough of your revolting talk, Olaf," he said sternly. "We've caught you now, and there's no way you'll be getting away. The Lake Lachrymose Police Department will be happy to capture a known criminal wanted for fraud, murder, and the endangerment of children."

"And arson," Count Olaf piped up.

"*I said that's enough,*" Mr. Poe growled. Count Olaf, the Baudelaire orphans, and even the massive creature looked surprised that Mr. Poe had spoken so sternly. "You have preyed upon these children for the last time, and I am making absolutely sure that you are handed over to the proper authorities. Disguising yourself won't work. Telling lies won't work. In fact there's nothing at all you can do about your situation."

"Really?" Count Olaf said, and his filthy lips curved up in a smile. "I can think of something that I can do."

"And what," said Mr. Poe, "is that?"

Count Olaf looked at each one of the Baudelaire orphans, giving each one a smile as if the children were tiny chocolates he was saving to eat for later. Then he smiled at the massive creature, and then, slowly, he smiled at Mr. Poe. "I can run," he said, and ran. Count Olaf ran, with the massive creature lumbering behind him, in the direction of the heavy metal gate.

"Get back here!" Mr. Poe shouted. "Get back here in the name of the law! Get back here in the name of justice and righteousness! Get back here in the name of Mulctuary Money Management!"

"We can't just shout at them!" Violet shouted. "Come on! We have to chase them!"

"I'm not going to allow children to chase after a man like that," Mr. Poe said, and called out again, "Stop, I say! Stop right there!"

"We can't let them escape!" Klaus cried. "Come on, Violet! Come on, Sunny!"

"No, no, this is no job for children," Mr. Poe said. "Wait here with your sisters, Klaus. I'll retrieve them. They won't get away from Mr. Poe. *You, there! Stop!*"

"But we can't wait here!" Violet cried. "We have to get into a sailboat and look for Aunt Josephine! She may still be alive!"

"You Baudelaire children are under my care," Mr. Poe said firmly. "I'm not going to let small children sail around unaccompanied."

"But if we hadn't sailed unaccompanied," Klaus pointed out, "we'd be in Count Olaf's clutches by now!"

"That's not the point," Mr. Poe said, and began to walk quickly toward Count Olaf and the creature. "The point is—"

But the children didn't hear the point over the loud *slam!* of the tall metal gate. The creature had slammed it shut just as Mr. Poe had reached it.

"Stop immediately!" Mr. Poe ordered, calling through the gate. "Come back here, you unpleasant person!" He tried to open the tall gate and found it locked. "It's locked!" he cried to the children. "Where is the key? We must find the key!"

The Baudelaires rushed to the gate but stopped as they heard a jingling sound. "I have the key," said Count Olaf's voice, from the other side of the gate. "But don't worry. I'll see you soon, orphans. *Very soon.*"

"Open this gate immediately!" Mr. Poe

shouted, but of course nobody opened the gate. He shook it and shook it, but the spiky metal gate never opened. Mr. Poe hurried to a phone booth and called the police, but the children knew that by the time help arrived Count Olaf would be long gone. Utterly exhausted and more than utterly miserable, the Baudelaire orphans sank to the ground, sitting glumly in the very same spot where we found them at the beginning of this story.

In the first chapter, you will remember, the Baudelaires were sitting on their suitcases, hoping that their lives were about to get a little bit better, and I wish I could tell you, here at the end of the story, that it was so. I wish I could write that Count Olaf was captured as he tried to flee, or that Aunt Josephine came swimming up to Damocles Dock, having miraculously escaped from the Lachrymose Leeches. But it was not so. As the children sat on the damp ground, Count Olaf was already halfway across the lake and would soon be on board a train, disguised as a rabbi to fool the police, and I'm sorry to tell you that he was already concocting another scheme to steal the Baudelaire fortune. And we can never know exactly what was happening to Aunt Josephine as the children sat on the dock, unable to help her, but I will say that eventually—about the time when the Baudelaire orphans were forced to attend a miserable boarding school—two fishermen found both of Aunt Josephine's life jackets, all in tatters and floating alone in the murky waters of Lake Lachrymose.

In most stories, as you know, the villain would be defeated, there would be a happy ending, and everybody would go home knowing the moral of the story. But in the case of the Baudelaires everything was wrong. Count Olaf, the villain, had not succeeded with his evil plan, but he certainly hadn't been defeated, either. You certainly couldn't say that there was a happy ending. And the Baudelaires could not go home knowing the moral of the story, for the simple reason that they could not go home at all. Not only had Aunt Josephine's house fallen into the lake, but the Baudelaires' real home—the house where they had lived with their parents—was just a pile of ashes in a vacant lot, and they couldn't go back there no matter how much they wanted to.

But even if they could go home it would be difficult for me to tell you what the moral of the story is. In some stories, it's easy. The moral of "The Three Bears," for instance, is "Never break into someone else's house." The moral of "Snow White" is "Never eat apples." The moral of World War One is "Never assassinate Archduke Ferdinand." But Violet, Klaus, and Sunny sat on the dock and watched the sun come up over Lake Lachrymose and wondered exactly what the moral was of their time with Aunt Josephine.

The expression "It dawned on them," which I am about to use, does not have anything to do with the sunlight spreading out over Damocles

Dock. "It dawned on them" simply means "They figured something out," and as the Baudelaire orphans sat and watched the dock fill with people as the business of the day began, they figured out something that was very important to them. It dawned on them that unlike Aunt Josephine, who had lived up in that house, sad and alone, the three children had one another for comfort and support over the course of their miserable lives. And while this did not make them feel entirely safe, or entirely happy, it made them feel appreciative.

"Thank you, Klaus," Violet said appreciatively, "for figuring out that note. And thank you, Sunny, for stealing the keys to the sailboat. If it weren't for the two of you we would now be in Count Olaf's clutches."

"Thank you, Violet," Klaus said appreciatively, "for thinking of the peppermints to gain us some time. And thank you, Sunny, for biting the peg leg just at the right moment. If it weren't for the two of you, we would now be doomed."

"Pilums," Sunny said appreciatively, and her siblings understood at once that she was thanking Violet for inventing the signaling device, and thanking Klaus for reading the atlas and guiding them to Curdled Cave.

They leaned up against one another appreciatively, and small smiles appeared on their damp and anxious faces. They had each other. I'm not sure that "The Baudelaires had each other" is the moral of this story, but to the three siblings it was enough. To have each other in the midst of their unfortunate lives felt like having a sailboat in the middle of a hurricane, and to the Baudelaire orphans this felt very fortunate indeed.

LEMONY SNICKET was born before you were and is likely to die before you as well. A studied expert in rhetorical analysis, Mr. Snicket has spent the last several eras researching the travails of the Baudelaire orphans. His findings are being published serially by Harper-Collins.

Visit him on the Web at http://www.harperchildrens.com/lsnicket/ *or E-mail to* lsnicket@harpercollins.com

BRETT HELQUIST was born in Ganado, Arizona, grew up in Orem, Utah, and now lives in New York City. He earned a bachelor's degree in fine arts from Brigham Young University and has been illustrating ever since. His art has appeared in many publications, including *Cricket* magazine and *The New York Times*.

To My Kind Editor,

I am writing to you from the Paltryville
Town Hall, where I have convinced the mayor
to allow me inside the eye-shaped office of
Dr. Orwell in order to further investigate
what happened to the Baudelaire orphans
while they were living in the area.

Next Friday, a black jeep will be in
the northwest corner of the parking lot
of the Orion Observatory. Break into it.
In the glove compartment, you should find
my description of this frightening chapter
in the Baudelaires' lives, entitled THE
MISERABLE MILL, as well as some information
on hypnosis, a surgical mask, and sixty-
eight sticks of gum. I have also included
the blueprint of the pincher machine, which
I believe Mr. Helquist will find useful for
his illustrations.

Remember, you are my last hope that
the tales of the Baudelaire orphans can
finally be told to the general public.

With all due respect,

Lemony Snicket

Lemony Snicket